Prairie Schooner Book Prize in Fiction   *Editor*: Hilda Raz

Our Lady of the
ARTICHOKES

AND OTHER PORTUGUESE-AMERICAN STORIES

Katherine Vaz

UNIVERSITY OF NEBRASKA PRESS · LINCOLN AND LONDON

Acknowledgment for the use of previously published
material appears on p. xi, which constitutes an
extension of the copyright page. The photographs
"The Holy Ghost Cape on the Ground," "The
Artichoke Scene," "The Holy Ghost Cape with
Attendants," and "The Net Mural," all by Michael
Trudeau, are reproduced with permission; the photograph "Pear in Bottle" is used with the permission
of Susan Seubert/Botanica/jupiterimages, 475 Park
Avenue South, 4th Floor, New York, New York,
10016 / (800) 764-7427. All other photographs
courtesy of the author.

The writing of this book was supported in part by
The Radcliffe Institute for Advanced Study at Harvard University and the MacDowell Artists Colony
in Peterborough, New Hampshire.

Library of Congress Cataloging-in-Publication Data

Vaz, Katherine.
Our lady of the artichokes and other Portuguese-
American stories / Katherine Vaz.
p. cm.—(Prairie Schooner book prize in fiction)
ISBN 978-0-8032-1790-4 (pbk.: alk. paper)
1. Portuguese Americans—Fiction. I. Title.
PS3572.A97O87 2008
813'.54—dc22   2008009969

Set in Galliard.
Designed by Ashley Muehlbauer.

For my Christopher

When I die, my son,
Let me be the child, the little one.
Pick me up in your arms
And carry me into your house.
Undress my tired and human self
And tuck me into your bed.
If I wake up, tell me stories
So that I'll fall back asleep.
And give me your dreams to play with
Until the dawning of that day
You know will dawn.

—"One midday in late spring"
by Fernando Pessoa

Contents

Acknowledgments

The stories in this collection first appeared—some in slightly different form—in the following publications: "Taking a Stitch in a Dead Man's Arm" in *BOMB Magazine* 77 (Fall 2001); "All Riptides Roar with Sand from Opposing Shores" in *Notre Dame Review* 21 (Winter 2006); "Our Lady of the Artichokes" in *Pleiades* 24, no. 1 (2004); "My Bones Here Are Waiting for Yours" in *Five Points* 8, no. 3 (2004); "The Man Who Was Made of Netting" in *Tin House* 2, no. 2 (Winter 2001), reprinted as a bilingual book with the title *O Homen Que Era Feito de Rede*, translated by Vamberto Freitas and illustrated by Álamo Oliveira (Lisbon: Edições ASA, 2002); "The Knife Longs for the Ruby" in *Ninth Letter* 1, no. 1 (Spring-Summer 2004); and "Lisbon Story" in *Harvard Review* 30 (Spring 2006). Special thanks to Christina Thompson for her invaluable editing of "Lisbon Story."

The epigraph is from "One midday in late spring" by Fernando Pessoa, from *A Little Larger than the Entire Universe*, trans. Richard Zenith, copyright © 2006 by Richard Zenith. Used by permission of Penguin, a division of Penguin Group (USA) Inc.

The writing of this book was supported in part by The Radcliffe Institute for Advanced Study at Harvard University and the MacDowell Artists Colony; I am deeply grateful for their generosity. Thanks also to Michael Trudeau for the use of several of his beautiful photos.

 *Fatherless*

Taking a Stitch in a Dead Man's Arm

I changed the bandage over my father's knee in the final month of his life. His wound was violet, and blood pulsed through. I never looked away from it. I swallowed my vomit when it struck the back of my clenched teeth; I was ready to swallow my insides as often as necessary—it was important to gaze at his flesh exactly as it was because I would not have it with me for much longer. I wanted to learn matter-of-factness about being this close to someone. The yellow fluid on the gauze around the bloodstains, the cortisone spray that would have made Papa scream if he'd had the strength: my stain, my shock, and my scream.

A brain lesion gave him double vision. Everything wore a register of itself, a crown of haze. It amused him to watch people walking around with the ghosts of themselves stuck to their skins. Papa's knee had ripped open when he fell off a ladder while trying to repair a broken window sash. Frantic to protect us, to seal every entry, he had crawled from his sickbed while my mother was at work at the Sunshine Biscuit factory and I was at school. A killer who called himself the Zodiac was roaming the Bay Area. He was sending letters with obscene ciphers to the *San Francisco Chronicle*.

"Isabel," said my father, his fingers brushing first the specter of my face and then my face. The rind of the moon cut through the window-pane. The wallpaper was an old pattern of "The Strawberry Thief," with sharp birds poking through tall red grasses. Saint Anthony of love and lost things had an arm span covering half the top of the bureau, and someone had sent over a plug-in picture, with a lightbulb in the back, of Saint Lucy with her plate of eyeballs. Papa was forty-two; he would stay posed in time with black hair. He did not know how to guard me anymore. He could no longer hide the newspapers, as he had when Richard Speck murdered those nurses in Chicago. *Fear gives off a smell. That's how evil finds its victims, Isabel. If you don't give it off, you'll be safe, you won't get hurt in the dark.*

I told him he must stop worrying. The Zodiac would not bother coming to our town: what was here? Every morning I walked to the boulevard to catch the bus to Bishop Delancy High School in Oakland, and we passed the Adobe Feed Store, where my father had said that hiding in the sacks were eggs, smaller than the eye could see, waiting to hatch into vermin. And sometimes I had caught it, in the days of holding his hand when we went to buy chicken scratch. The sacks jumped, they stirred a bit, moth wings straining against the weight of the feed. Eggs and wings: I thought of death as white. Our morning bus passed the Miniature Golden-Tee, with its hydra-head of neon dragons guarding the windmills, clowns with big mouths waiting for a golf ball to gag them, and a little Wild West corral with a gate that gave out a horse whinny again and again as it swung open. What was in San Damiano? It sounds like a place with terra-cotta earth and a Spanish mission, but it was an ordinary suburb, house after house with those netless basketball hoops, with a gauntlet of stores on San Damiano Boulevard. People favored wind chimes in the shape of pagodas, which they bought in Chinatown in San Francisco, as if crossing the bridge was go-ing from part A of the world to part B, and the winds blew in and tilted the pagodas and no one ever straightened them; there was always a faint music, a trickle, really, coming from these shattered columns of pagodas.

I was in love with someone who was leaving me his own lessons in being unafraid. James was a tall Filipino boy in my sophomore class who wore three-piece business suits on Free Dress Day and smoked cigars with the Asian kids in the parking lot, and once when Sonny Barger and some Hells Angels rode through, as they did now and then, James threw a flaming butt end at one of them and got flipped off but not hurt. I understood that the motorcyclist admired James for a moment, and it thrilled me, to watch how someone could go straight toward points of fear.

Violet Wong, my best friend, would get onto the bus with me at the San Damiano stop, and she'd take out the green eye shadow she'd stolen from her mother. We'd put it on with our fingers, and my lashes were so long that they stroked green dust onto the inside of my glasses. She wanted to help me be beautiful for James. I had written a speech for him, and he won the regional Lions Club contest with it and would go on to the state finals. He had not told me that he won; one of his friends did, and when I went to him, he said, "I was going to tell you, Isabel." I wanted him to bury his face in my hair and wet my scalp with his mouth, to breathe my name back to me inside my ear.

How could I explain any of this to my father—the odd, awful timing of my love? *I'm not scared of anything, Papa.* That was all I could manage. "That's good!" he whispered. "I don't want you taking a stitch in my arm."

"No, I won't, Papa," I said, and we laughed.

It was a joke between us. When he was a boy on the island of São Miguel in the Azores, he suffered from a fear of the dark. His mother had explained to him that the cure for that in her family, she was very sorry to say, was taking a stitch in a dead man's arm. The cure was horrible, but its strength lasted forever. "Forever" had sounded wonderful to my father, so he said yes, next time there was a dead man in the town of Sete Cidades, he would take a stitch in his arm. Nothing could be worse than the monsters roving in his bedroom at night.

My father was five years old. His mother stood outside the chapel, crying into a lace handkerchief. Since fear of the dark is fear of aloneness, my father had to go by himself to the dead man in his casket. The thread in the needle was white. Papa thought the man looked like marzipan, especially where a drip of pink paint stood out on his ear. He had died from falling off a stone wall, where he had been entwining hydrangeas through the gaps. Everyone agreed that the world fought back when you tried to make it beautiful.

My father pulled up the young dead man's cuff and touched a waxy arm. His name was Fernando, and his mustache was trimmed neatly for the first time ever. My father stuck the needle into the wrist and pushed until it dipped through flesh and emerged from under the skin, and then he thought, All right, that's enough. Two drops of fluid seeped at the prick marks. My father's stomach shrank smaller than a fist. He left the thread in the man's skin and drew his sleeve down and ran back to his mother.

It was easy to give up fear of darkness rather than repeat such a cure. Maybe it was some Old World remnant, sticking a man with a needle to make certain that he was not merely in a coma. At one funeral in Sete Cidades, a man had bolted upright in his coffin while being borne to the cemetery and roared, "How will I breathe underground?" Maybe the idea was to stitch the body to earth, so that it would not cling with its worms to the spirit trying to fly to heaven.

Death sinks a person's eyes back until they become bright creatures in a tide pool. I got up to go to my room, and my father grabbed my arm and said, "Don't leave me, Isabel! Not yet," and I saw, in the gleam of fever, in the water on his eyes, a terrible fear, and I did not know if it might be from him or if it were my own, reflecting back to me. Perhaps I was so far into fright that I'd touched clear round to the other side, where I could claim to be past it; perhaps I was a

Suddenly the dark drifted into a white blindness, like the belly of a night turned inside out. I got up in the white sac of night to clean the green leather couch, Comet on a rag that made the green pale. The majolica Christ child over the stove, inside His ring of majolica fruit, had collected streaks of grease, too far to reach.

I piled bedclothes on top of myself and put my arms and legs around them and thought of them as a man, and I thrust around like a stupid fish on land, and that made me feel worse, because a man would move in ways beyond predicting. Even then I suspected that when a woman got to be experienced in love, that was the point—for him to surprise you; the very touch of love was a plunging reminder of the unknown, the same unknown I carried with me now.

I heard that James came in third in the state finals of the speech contest held by the Lions Club. I was about to round the corner to find him at his locker, to tell him that he had gone quite far with my speech and should not think of it as failing. I decided this would not violate my vow to give him up. I stopped when I heard his voice say, "Deborah, I'm dying to fuck you." And thereafter I saw him with this girl, who had long blond hair that she plaited and undid so that it held a ripple. Her rouge compact fell out of her purse in the bathroom, and I kept it: Mauve Turbulence.

In religion class Sister Miriam showed a filmstrip about sex, in which a priest's voice-over affixed every act of physical love onto a scale. "Looking at, talking to, walking with" was at the end marked "Early Stage of Arousal." "S.I."—for "sexual intercourse"—was at the far other end, in the Marriage part of the scale. The projector went Ping! whenever Sister Miriam had to move the filmstrip. The narrating priest said cheerily, "I really don't know where to put the fondling of the breasts!" and the screen showed an "f" surrounded by question marks that ended up straddling the line between Engagement and Marriage.

So God was merely amused. I had not even been on the scale with

liar; I could stand that. But I could not bear to think that the fear might be coming from him.

For once I did not mind Momma's habit every night of getting out our glow-in-the-dark rosary set. The Holy Family statue had a hollow compartment to house the rosary. I held it under a lamp's light to turn the beads into glowworms. My mother snapped off the lights, and she, my father, and I handed the fluorescent beads from one grasp to another in the dark. Fingering this string of lights like the souls of infant stars, I finally knew what to pray: *I'll give up love, if You'll save my father.*

That was my bargain with God.

Our Alameda County transit bus, #80, went from San Damiano through San Leandro and then under the "Free Huey" banners along East 14th Street into Oakland. Near the General Motors plant, we picked up the riders going to Castlemont High, near Bishop Delancy. They had Afros with Fro-Piks stuck in them and wore Angela Davis glasses and hip-hugger lace-up football pants, including the girls, with angel-flight hems. On their Pee-Chee folders they had penciled dashikis and black-haloed hair over the Waspy white kids in tennis outfits. We lifted our schoolbooks onto our laps to free up seats for them.

One day Charles Mayer, a Castlemont Knight with his purple-and-white letterman's jacket, sat next to me. Everyone knew him from his picture in the newspaper. He was heading for the NBA. He ripped out a sheet of binder paper from a notebook and began writing in pencil. Out of the corner of my eye I saw his writing, and I did not know what came over me when I leaned over and said, "No, 'receive' is 'ei,' not 'ie.'"

I cringed when he said, "What?" and looked right at me. I glanced near his eyes and told him about the spelling of "receive." He jotted it down and insisted it didn't look right, but I told him, Believe me, I'm sorry for speaking to you, I didn't mean it, but I'm telling you the truth: receive.

Charles Mayer handed me his paper and said, "What else is wrong here? Tell me."

Every day after that, I moved my books for him to sit where I could help with his homework. Once when some Castlemont kids pried up a bus seat and crammed it out a window to protest the arrest of Eldridge Cleaver, and the Delancy kids were jostled around, Charles Mayer told them not to touch me. It had nothing to do with the usual sort of love; that was understood. He had a girlfriend and plenty of other girls after him. I was ugly, with my skinniness and battles against fright. We all rolled our red herringbone tweed skirts at the waist in a gruesome attempt to make them miniskirts. He was taking a portion of my mind, but not as James had. One morning Charles handed me five pralines made by his grandmother, in a baggie secured with a psychedelic-streaked rubber band.

He said, "Thanks—tell me your name?"

"Isabel Dias," I said.

"Isabel Dias," he said, as if pleased with locating an obscure country on a map. "I got a B on my essay about my future," he said.

My hand was moist around the bag with the pralines. "Thank you," I said.

"No problem, thank *you*," he said, and we each turned back to our books.

In that essay he had written: *This is my world at this moment. Everyone I meet is my history. This is the year that Charles Mayer has stepped into his life.*

When we disembarked at Delancy, Violet said, "What's wrong, Isabel?" I ran to the restroom, willing to let the smokers beat me silly, and I locked myself into a stall and wept. I wept without making noise, I was good at that; imagine me counting just a tiny bit as someone's history. How uncanny, too, that my father should seep inside my lonely hours: with the raw instincts of a small animal, with the Zodiac on the loose, I had found myself a protector on the bus, a guardian angel on his way to money and fame, far, far above anything

I was, but I counted now in his tally of moments, owing to my of fear in spelling out *Receive*.

An essay or two later, Charles Mayer stopped taking our bus. I ne saw him in person again, though I continued to see his photo in t sports news. I heard that he had a car now. Rumor had it that it w a gift from a recruiter because his future was so much on the rise.

I studied my mother the way I looked at the eyes and blood of m father, to preserve her as she was right then, down to the safflowe oil with its faint scent that she rubbed into her skin. Already, still young, her skin was overly set, like the gel on a photo negative, and her light brown hair was thinning, and her glance seemed not to be owning things but making blank spaces where she looked, and I forgave her, I never thought that not seeing me meant that she did not love me. She could hardly bear to look at my father. I would make watery soup but she refused it. Right through her skin it was poking out, the dryness in her bones. When she curled up next to my father on their bed, I took off her shoes and set them upright on the carpet, where they exhaled her entire day of standing and picking the pink marshmallow cookies off the conveyor belt and putting them bottom to bottom inside the compartments of a box. The Sunshine people let the workers eat all they wanted, but one week we had devoured four boxes of pink cookies and three boxes of Sunshine cheese crackers on purpose, to break the habit of wanting any more.

Momma, dozing next to my father, would give a startled shudder of remembering me, and with her eyes still shut, not looking at either of us for fear of dying of it, she let me crawl between her and Papa. Their silver carpet was bare, stripped to its gums. Somehow the roses on the carpet had worn themselves onto the bottoms of our shoes, but since we saw no roses on our shoes I think they must have gone up into our feet, roses inside my mother's feet and climbing inside her sore calves as she stood at the factory.

When I roused myself to go off to my own bed, I could not sleep.

James. I had not owned this love enough for me to offer it up. And the pain I was in meant I had not even truly surrendered the nothing I had. But what of any of it? My father might be saved now, but there comes a time when such a prayer is always laughed at.

My lungs flattened so that it was impossible to get air into the bellows of them. I took an early bus home and crawled onto the bed where my father lay with his pounding double vision. I did not speak; I tried to get some breath into me so I would not die. He put his hand on my hair—kindly, though I had failed him. My glasses fell off and the birds on the wall, the strawberry thieves, blurred into a red ironworks; it was almost pretty. He said that he'd been wrong his whole life; taking a stitch in a dead man's arm hadn't been about fear of the dark.

Was I listening to him? Was I?

I moved a shoulder a bit to signal him yes.

It was about leaving behind the curse of waiting. "Waiting is the fear you have to get over, Isabel," said my father, so lightly I barely heard him. It frightened me that he could hear my heart battering its way onto the sheet. "Don't wait for anyone." Because waiting was darkness, having no imagination to see beyond the fallen curtain, where you were right then. But when you were young and looking at a dead man, and actually sticking it to him, you were saying that it wasn't your time to die, it was your time to enter your better and better future.

There were so many cracks in our house that I was sure that water ebbed in while we slept, filling every room to the ceiling. The Zodiac got in through one of the cracks but we fought him, and his knife, instead of killing us, opened gills on our sides and we could breathe.

The Zodiac had a fear of drowning and swam away. My mirrored vanity plate of lavender soaps and vanilla cologne got swept up in a vortex of water. My father had been a champion ocean swimmer, and this, to him, was child's play. This was nothing, getting to dance

9

underwater until morning, when the water receded and daylight began and a string of water was coming out of our mouths, connecting whatever had gone on in our heads in the night to our pillows.

My mother and I threw out the newspapers, though my father could no longer read. We had to protect him from the latest: the Zodiac had written a letter that said: *Ha! Ha! Ha! Your pigs can't catch me!! When a busload of Catholic kiddies step off in their uniforms I'll go pop! pop! and I am going to find me some niggers, too.*

My #80 bus, with Delancy and Castlemont students, was a gift box, wrapped and delivered, for the Zodiac. Everyone thought this, but no one figured we should worry. The Zodiac would stay in San Francisco. Surely death would not trouble itself to stalk us on this one obscure line from San Damiano to Oakland.

Death was too busy, death was in my father's body. I stitched my gaze to my father's when he yelled, "Isabel!" He looked straight into me, and I looked back, into the iris and nerves.

When he died my mother insisted on a simple, closed-coffin affair, no flinging ourselves at the dead, no kisses that drew back embalming paint. But at his wake I almost fainted from the smell of the casseroles, the Chinese noodles baked over ground beef and peas, the lasagnas oozing like a cutaway of magnified muscle, the Boston cream pies leaking their middles—I stopped eating for days, and then, all at once, my bones shook as if my father were shaking me, I saw black puddles moving along the floor and sticking together to make odd black-water animals, and I could not wait to eat; I ate, my mother said, like someone who was going to be shot in the morning.

As a girl I had attended a school run by Carmelite nuns from Spain who told us stories about their parents being killed in the civil war. Once a year we filed into the convent's chapel and the priest held out a black speck housed under a glass swollen like a belly. We had to kiss the glass over this black jot, which was a particle of bone from the founder of the order.

How had this bone chip been obtained? What part of the body was it from?

Why did we turn the color of night down to our bones when we died?

There is always some way in which we lend ourselves to taking a stitch in the body of the dead. Someone had taken not a needle but a knife and carved into bones; I, for my part, had long ago stitched my breath to the glass over a fragment of a woman.

At school Violet said, "Isabel! Did you know that *all* sounds *ever* spoken stay on the waves hiding inside the air?"

And so I stepped outdoors until the blue sky bent to find me, to hold a curve against my ears that was my father saying, *Here I am, my dear, for my love for you is not merely in one world but all worlds.* It would be just like him to find a way to speak barely above a breeze; it had to be gentle because it was for me. And when birds flew with inclined wings, the air that planed off their feathers said, *Do not wait. Fear nothing.*

My mother would sit in dark rooms and not move. In the living room the dotted Swiss curtains bulged out when air blew in through the screens. It was as if the air had shape, and the curtains were stretching themselves over it. "Shall we go for a walk, Momma?" I asked, and out we ventured under the birds in the sky, stunned and silent, but at a distance I imagine we must have seemed to be striding quite fearlessly down the road. I could not rescue my father, but for now I could rescue her: I had won my bargain, it seemed; I had kept my father with me.

While walking down Redwood Road to the bus stop on San Damiano Boulevard, I noticed a car—maybe a station wagon—going in one driveway, pulling out, going into the driveway of the next house, pulling out. Someone was following me, entering and idling for a moment in every driveway so that he could stay behind me. I walked a little faster and stepped closer to the curb. Hardly any other cars were out at that hour, still dark, just after six. I was wearing my trench coat over my uniform, with the fringe of my herringbone skirt showing, and red knee socks and coffee-and-cream saddle shoes.

I passed the San Damiano Library, a low glass building across from Faith Lutheran Church; the car went into its parking lot. I thought that if I took care not to look at the car, it would leave me alone. I tried a fast walk, afraid to look over my shoulder until I told myself, Fear nothing, your father is with you. Don't give off the smell of fear; that's when the larger animal will catch the smaller one. I knew how to protect myself. The boulevard wasn't far, and men worked all hours at the Union 76 station near the bus stop. I wondered if I should get the license plate number or look at the man behind the wheel, but I broke into a run when I saw the gas station.

Our A.C. Transit bus driver, Owen Campbell, was getting coffee out of the vending machine. When I ran up to him, breathing hard, I said, "There's a car back there I don't like."

Mr. Campbell and two of the station attendants walked out with me and looked down the street, but the car had vanished.

"You get the number?" asked Mr. Campbell.

I shook my head. I told him what had happened, and he put his hand on my shoulder and said, "Maybe it's just one of those things."

"Maybe," I said.

"Because it's a strange world," he said.

"That's right."

He escorted me to his bus. I told Violet that someone had come after me in my Catholic uniform, and she stifled a yell and started a whisper in the bus about the Zodiac. By the time we stopped at the General Motors plant for the Castlemont students, the fear went into their skin, too, and they picked up the murmur: of course he'd find us. We're a two-for-one deluxe murderer's dream. The girl next to me opened her Bible to the Twenty-third Psalm: *He leadeth me beside the still waters/Yea, though I walk through the valley of the shadow of death, I will fear no evil.*

She took hold of my sleeve. We did not speak, but she clutched these stitches all over my arm. I hope it made her less afraid. For me it was a sweetness out of nowhere. How close to dying it still arrives, the better and better surprise. We could be minutes from gunfire, and someone finds the time to take hold of me.

When the bus stopped at Delancy, Mr. Campbell opened the door and exited first. He turned around and walked a bit, and then I stepped off. If the car were lurking I would be able to identify it. It was the most fearless moment of my life. When I was out in the open, and the other students poured out, Mr. Campbell said to me, "God bless you, sweetheart," a further gift in the middle of all that fear. No one had ever called me sweetheart before, not even in my family.

There was no news that day, nor on any of the following days, about the Zodiac killer. He was never found, though it was suggested that some prisoner, apprehended for other crimes, might be hugging to himself the secret of how he had terrorized us. Who knows? We refuse to believe in the persistence of the sinister. Perhaps he is a clerk or a dental technician or a professor, his skull's interior filled with webs that no one else can see.

Violet Wong drowned in the Bay during a marine biology trip in her freshman year at the University of California at Berkeley.

As far as I know, Charles Mayer never made it to the NBA; I hope life has not disappointed him. I hope he did not die in Vietnam. I wish him a good and cheerful family.

James came into my life again twenty years after I had last seen him, at an awards banquet for journalists. I was getting a small prize for some pictures I had taken. I was divorced and madly, utterly, out of my skin in love with a married man. I lived in a studio on Pine Street in San Francisco, where I developed pictures in my own darkroom. James came up to me at the banquet, and we had a drink together. But he was no longer beautiful to me, because he reminded me of what I still was—someone perpetually learning not to wait forever. There are times that contain all we shall ever be; everything we learn

13

can be traced back to that start of the shading in of all we more fully come to know. Back then in the last year of my father, when I learned to step into my life, there lay the first threads: darkness, waiting, the dragon in the landscape, love running in blood and water through my grasp.

My mother still lives in our little house with the red wallpaper in San Damiano, the sort of artless place that no one wants to admit being from, the place where I thought, What was here?

With Andrew, my married man, I gave up many things, including my notion of "here." When he came to where I lived—here, there, it didn't matter at all—anywhere was everything. He knew how to kiss the length of my spine and enter me almost at the same time and hold my head from behind so that he could feel my violent heaving face, and when I was by myself, when he went home to his wife, I was quite clear about one definite new fright. I had crested something and hit up against that farthest fear of the dark: nothing would touch me more than this that I was about to lose. Soon he and I would end this passion simply because it refused to have an end of its own. You could take a stitch in a dead man's arm in order to defeat the night, because you wanted to live. But what if you hit up against a love that would cling to you, so that no one else would be able to touch you directly, not ever again, because that—him, it, the hours, this created thing between you—would stay adhered?

Oh, Father. One lifetime is never enough to figure everything out, not the mystery you left off solving, the mystery that began when you were very young and took a stitch in the body of death and thought: *There it is, I've finished, I will never again be afraid of the dark.* What happens when it's you that's the body lying there alone?

All Riptides Roar with Sand from Opposing Shores

May 1, 1963
Hayward, California

Dear Lúcia,

I hope you will answer us. Oh, please! My friends (Alice & Maria) at Transfiguration School have asked me to write to you. They say my penmanship is nice. I disagree with some of the Palmer Method shapes such as how to do a "J," but Sister Delfina says that if I imagine the loops make half a butterfly I might like it and do as I'm told.

We want to know why you won't release the Third Secret that Mary gave you at Fátima. Sister Delfina says the Pope has it and he won't tell us. How bad could it be? We are dying of curiosity and maybe you just need to be asked politely.

The other (real) reason Alice & Maria want me to write is that I have a true story that is close to you. My great-aunt, Mariana Sousa Batista de Pereira, lived nearby when the miracle happened to you. Except that Tia Mariana didn't hear or see Our Lady like you did. I never met this great-aunt, but my father keeps a picture of her in his study. She's been dead a while. Did you meet her? My father says yes, because where you came from was very small before you made it famous.

Forgive me for writing in English, but I've learned only a few words in Portuguese. My father grew up in Lisbon but came to California when he was ten. We could ask him for help, but he will probably say, "Don't bother her!" My mother was born in Wisconsin. Her grandparents were from Holland, Italy, and Denmark. My dad fixes the cable cars in San Francisco! He met my mother when she was a tourist riding on the hills to get a view of the water, the bridge, and the prison (Alcatraz).

Do you have people who can translate and answer your mail? We're sure you must get a lot of letters.

We do not know anyone who talks directly to heaven and we are not jealous, just impressed!

Please tell us the secret.

What do you do all day (and night)?

OK! Bye! We love you!

Your friends,

Lara Pereira
Alice Nicolini
Maria Hathaway

Exma. Sóror Maria Lúcia of the Discalced Carmelites,
Pontevedra, Portugal:

Happy 57th birthday. I sent a letter almost a year ago and
waited & waited and never heard back. Did I offend you? I
should have written your full title and name. I am sorry. I still
would please like to hear the Third Secret.

Did you pray for President Kennedy when he was killed? A
picture of him is hanging next to Jesus and the Pope on the wall
of our dining room. My dad has covered Kennedy with black
cloth.

I read in your memoir that your father's nickname was
The Pumpkin, and that you loved fancy clothing when you
were my age. You wore gold earrings that hung below your
shoulders (amazing) and a hat with feathers from a peacock
pinned together with beads that made a castle on your head.
You played a game called Buttons under a plum tree and ate
the berries that grew on the roots of yellow bellflowers. Gold &
shiny blue & plum & yellow. You sound beautiful!

I am tall and thin (like you) & my skin is milk-colored (like
my mother's), but my eyes are a weird violet--it's a mystery
where they're from. I invented them! My hair is black like
my father's, and very long and straight. A banty hen, honey-
colored, lives in our yard, and I glued one of her feathers to a
barrette. We own a fig tree. Dad showed me how to cut a cross
in the bottom of a fig with a penknife and turn the insides
outward so the fig changes into a purple starfish. He teaches
me everything because I have no brothers or sisters.

What are you doing for your birthday? I stole my mother's
lipstick (Scarlet Surprise) and painted it on myself, and when

I finish writing, I'm going to press my lips hard on the page. I thought about what to send for your birthday that would fit in an envelope. Please take my mouth! Because colors like plum and gold thrilled you and Mary made the sun fling out a rainbow so that people would believe you were telling the truth about talking to her, but now you're wrapped only in black and white. You may put my red mouth against yours and then lift my letter away and then put it against you again and so on and so on so that I can kiss kiss kiss you. & you can Wear Me.

Alice isn't friends with us so much anymore, and Maria is afraid of pestering you but asks me to say hello.

Your (patiently waiting) friend,

Lara Pereira
& Maria Hathaway, who isn't here but wants to be included
& My Red Kiss:

March 4, 1970
Hayward, California

Dear Sister Lúcia,

My father is gone. I'm in pieces. A priest here at Bishop Delancy High School had the NERVE to suggest that my father is in hell because of how he died. That priest should burn in hell next to my mother, who ran off with a lawyer to Portland

& I never want to speak to her again, not that she's crying for me either. I WON'T live with my father's sister, Tia Palmira, who resides in trash-heap Hayward. She ALSO believes my dad is in hell & REFUSES to let me say his name! A gaggle of my relatives decided that fifteen is too young to be on my own ("in these hippie times") so they're packing me off TO MACAU! I had to look it up on a map!! Some wheezebag of an aunt there will take me in & at this point, great, I don't care. Les Relatives tried to cheer me up by gassing on and on about her owning a castle, big adventure, blah blah. They were only saying this because they claimed to have no room for me themselves. This Chinese Wonder Castle better have a drawbridge that I can pull up once I'm inside.

You're rude not to answer my letters. I can't believe there's no one to open your fan mail, read English, & stick your glossy photos into an envelope for those of us who don't GET miracles of our own.

I suppose if you're twelve and get to chat with the B.V.M., the thrills are downhill afterward. I think you dreamt up some supernatural fireworks and the world went bananas and you were in it too deep to back out. Come say hello if you're ever in Macau. Throw a rock over the moat against the drawbridge and maybe I'll hear you.

Forgive me. I'm awfully upset. Please—if it's true that you're joined with heaven, I'm begging you down to the flame that's in danger of going out in my soul . . . please put in a word for my father. He deserves lightness. My mother doesn't. She's in the middle of her new life in Portland. She pulverized my father's spirit and left us alone. One afternoon I opened the bathroom door and found him fully dressed within red and pink water in the tub. I dried him off and dressed him in his black cotton suit & lavender shirt & brocade vest (paisley seafoam green). He had the weight of water so it was a struggle for me, but I didn't mind. I trimmed his beard. The pink puckered satin inside his coffin looked like the wrinkles we all have as our brains. I kissed him good-bye in front of everyone. When they pulled me off him, I was wearing the paint on his face and I rubbed it into my skin and at last at last I got to be olive-dark like him.

Sincerely yours,

Miss Lara Pereira

June 19, 1979
Hayward, California

My dear Sister Lúcia,

My daughter's name is Blanca. She weighs five pounds (born a month early). Her spine is so light it's like soap bubbles held barely together. When she cries for me, her whole frame lurches, her face twists into a cactus flower.

I swore I wouldn't bother you again, but something in your memoir won't leave my mind. You were given a glimpse of Mary's celestial beauty in order to bear her showing you hell. You said that you kept your visions to yourself and preferred silence . . . because why describe eternal agony? I am beginning to understand. Heaven found me in Macau, in a house on Penha Hill. I can barely speak of it. David was twenty. He lived in my aunt's house; he was the offspring of her Chinese maid and my aunt's husband, who ran off to Shanghai when the baby arrived. The maid died in childbirth. My aunt raised the baby as her servant.

And then I appeared.

Since we were forbidden to converse, may I confess what we did?

We spoke in animals.

We stood at different corners of the house and our fingers moved like the legs of spiders spinning because we stored up a frenzy of longing for dusk so that our shadow plays could begin, his animals riding the turns of the dark and the light to arrive on an angle on my wall:

Mine forever, says the tiger.

I'll eat you up, replies the dog. (He taught me how to shape my hand and make a shadow-dog that could open its jaws.)

I'll turn huge, says the hare. I'll love you huge. A lurid flexing.

Unleash me, cries the dog. My skin is split and will take you in and where I roam your eyes will be inside mine.

The fish goes wild with: ride on my back and you will never drown!

I carry a seal of waiting on my forehead because of the boy who spoke to me in animals; he could not sneak into my room until midnight.

Lúcia, you've been sentenced to decades of hoping that Mary will visit you again . . . and she has not. Otherwise you'd share that with someone, wouldn't you?

David died. I'd have to say he died for me. He was shot and killed trying to swim to the mainland with a brooch stolen from my aunt. I was going to cross by land and meet him. He had to travel by water because the border connecting Macau to China is narrow and the guards strip everyone of valuables. We'd planned to sell the brooch on the other side.

I ran back to Hayward & rented a room I hardly left for three years & took in typing to survive. And then a new chapter opened: my husband's name is Ray Garcia; he's a chef. Blanca is his treasure and mine. In the small city that used to be called the Garden of Eden (ha!) thanks to the richness of the produce—artichokes, apricots, tomatoes, salt. The Hunts Cannery. Although these days my hometown is raggedy &

combustible & sharp-edged & semi-fruitless.

I sold a novel about my great-aunt Mariana who grew up near you & it earned me a teaching job fifty miles up the highway, at Redwood University. I am sending a signed copy to you. Tia Mariana's face in the photo my father owned had a crevice from her left eye to her chin, like a dry riverbed, a slash you could fall inside.

I am beginning to understand what it means that your cousin Francisco died of flu the year after he was present at the miracle. He got to hear but not see the gift from heaven. I sense him on the periphery of who I am now.

Cousin Jacinta was given the vision but not the words. She died young, too.

But you are required to go on and on in silence after tasting the full measure of everything.

So much of the way we pray turns into a demand that God the Father show His face at once and give us the list of what we want. Like children, we want creation handed to us, finished and polished, and when it is not as we wish it, we say the Father is dead and creation is not our concern. I am beginning to see that this is our own fear of learning how to love the world's mystery.

Here is a fragment of the Portuguese I retain: Sonhos cor-de-rosa. My father said this is how to wish someone sweet dreams: you call upon the tone the sky becomes when night joins day and the joining bleeds a little.

Pink dreams, Sister Lúcia . . . I must close. My child is waking.

Mrs. Lara Pereira Garcia

Dear Alice,

I roared with laughter at the clipping you sent from the
Enquirer! Sure, I wince, too, as I recall that letter we penned
when the nuns kept us in a death-grip of fear. Good heavens,
I can't decide what's funnier, the headline: "Revealed for
the 1st Time—the Third Secret of Fátima!" or the prophecy
itself. The apocalyptic has become so uniformly frothing and
dragonesque! Of course "millions of men will die from hour to
hour," and "fire and smoke will fall from the sky." What a lack of
specificity. I demand names, dates, places!

The highlight of this deathless prose concerns those Italian
reporters who leaked the Secret. How amusing that the Pope
couldn't stop himself from whispering the Big Secret Message
to his pal, Padre Pio. It's a chummy fame-game everywhere we
turn, including with the Heavenly Chosen, the Divinely Tapped
Club. (Remember how the nuns urged us to envy Padre Pio's
stigmata and power to read minds? The latter sounds pretty
good, I'll admit.)

The cult aspects surrounding miracles—especially this
one (ours)—make my skin crawl. Turn over a few bricks, and
out swarm the faithful, with their hoopla and anti-Communist
blather about Mary ordering us to pray for Russia. I'm not
the first to suggest that Lúcia may have entered that realm of
hysteria we'd prefer not to discuss, you know, sexual desire
sent down the wrong pipes and exploding out as garish
Technicolor paradise. (I should talk. With Gina two years old &
Blanca already six & with Ray working nights while I teach days
. . . well, you fill in that blank & what an aching blank it is.) Lúcia
also gets called a pious fraud who craved attention, but

there she earns my sympathy. Who can blame her for having enormous desires? Whatever was operating, she spilled it out, created a story, a refigured sky, an event that history will retain. Not bad. In the <u>Enquirer</u> picture, her skin seems utterly smooth for someone her age. Her eyelashes jet-black. I'll admit, Alice, that I've sent her a couple of letters over the years—she's never answered—but I see her as a woman alone who pierced herself with a few stunning, life-cracking hours. Isn't that what we all want? Without the religious dribble.

Yes, I published a second book. Poems. Sank like a stone. I am weary of teaching and may opt for a leave to chase after Gina. Blanca pretends I'm invisible.

It's good to be back in touch. Let's do better than annual Christmas cards. Send me broadcasts about Seattle & the boys & the ex-husband whenever (ha!) the spirit moves you.

Affectionately,

Lara

P.S. Did you hear that Maria earned a degree in nursing and moved to Guatemala? That was the last flash report I've gotten. Do you ever receive word from her?

Spring 2000
Pontevedra/Portugal

Dear Mrs. Lara Pereira Garcia,

My name is Helen Dodd. I am placing a "message into a bottle" and sending it. I am a journalist. Let me explain why I am here. I am not a Catholic. I was assigned to write an article for the <u>International Herald Tribune</u> about what the survivor of the Fátima event makes of the Vatican releasing this year the notes she was ordered to set down in 1944 of the so-called secret message from 1917. You may or may not have read this text now that it is public. I have since learned that fake versions have been surfacing for years. Nevertheless. My editor dispatched me to inquire as to her response to Cardinal Ratzinger's twelve-page commentary that suggested she may have "conjured her vision from devotional books." Ticklish stuff. He (the Cardinal certainly, and my editor probably) wishes to debunk without causing a riot. It stands to reason that three rural children at the end of World War I had a ready audience for a mass hallucination.

I met Lúcia, but not as I expected. An influx of mail this year, a magpie's nest of petitions now that the third secret is official, has staggered the convent. My being English-speaking seemed a godsend when I knocked at the convent's door, and I must have given off a whiff of the brisk and efficient. In exchange for agreeing to play secretary for a while (the pact rendered with effusive sign language), I was granted an audience with Lúcia. I didn't realize that this is unheard of. I hadn't even known her name before this year. I was escorted to her room and left to stand gaping like a fool at Lúcia in her bed. My grasp of the language is one tick shy of nil, but I was frankly relieved that I could not possibly question her reaction to a Cardinal who is hammering dents in her legacy.

She is 93. She needed a bath. I picked up a cloth from a basin on her nightstand and wiped her forehead. She sang a few notes that sounded like purring.

She was burning with fever. Her skin was inflamed. I began to sob. Lúcia put out her hands and held my face. Just like that, she put me back inside myself. Her fingernails have those ridges that indicate a lack of certain vitamins, but her eyes are a strong tint of brown. I was grateful. You see, my editor gave me this mission to "get me back in the game," because I lost my husband and son in a fire in New York. It happened a while ago, but I am stuck in time. I hail from Chicago but I'm not sure where I belong. My brothers and I went here and there. My father was a chemical engineer. New York was home for ten years, my entire marriage. My son was eight when our apartment burned, when he and Jeffrey were trapped. I was at a cocktail party at <u>Vogue</u>. I'd written captions for a fashion spread called "Masquerade." Jeffrey had a cold and agreed to watch Christopher. On my way home I bought orange juice for the morning. I arrived when they were pulling my husband from under a plank. I moved to Rome, followed by Madrid and Florida, which I disliked, and took assignments from newspapers. I share a flat in London now, but there's nothing to hold me there.

I am troubling you. I shall summarize by reporting that I've decided to tend to this old woman who is so hounded, as long as she agrees to have me. Though I hope to earn my keep by handling whatever mail I can decipher, it is impossible to deal with all of it. Five sheds hold stacks of decaying letters. The convent has haphazardly stored mail since 1975. Someone must have taken it upon herself to burn the backlog from 1917 to 1975. I decided to continue in that vein and get rid of most of the current 25-year backup. I was wrapping bunches in twine when yours dated 1979 fell out. The stamp was of Mona Lisa, and her beauty made me inhale sharply. Some bug had eaten part of your paper, and there was a brownish water stain.

I read about the boy you lost. I shall reveal that I cried for the both of us. You wrote in a manner that felt like the music I needed. When Christopher was small he had a menagerie of stuffed animals, and he made them chat with Jeffrey and me, and we talked back. It was such fun that I kept buying him animals.

You mentioned a husband and a daughter. It fills me with something that I would have called hope when I was younger. (I'm 42.)

Frequently the letters here are crazy, and I throw them out. Sometimes I give the photos tucked inside to Lúcia to touch, though I don't believe that does much. People never think to include a return envelope. This hunger for charms is sad but amusing. My favorite note was from a woman in Brighton, England, who wanted Lúcia to ask God to send her new linoleum for her kitchen.

I had gone to Fátima beforehand to do research, and I fainted. I hardly can hazard a theory as to what I expected. A blind gypsy was selling Band-Aids she had stolen from a truck. People were moaning and walking on their knees. I wanted to hoist them up and say, "Stop that immediately." Hired grannies were throwing wax body parts into the fire in a giant incinerator. I got close and looked. Candles were burning on iron rods set near the flames, and my stomach began to spin. Babies made out of wax, and breasts, legs, hearts, men's heads, burning. What a nightmare. I have no idea what it was all about, but now it's like a screen dropped over my vision.

I passed out. People thought I had been hit by God, because I drew an audience.

I ran off. First I bought a statue of Our Lady of Fátima, whose cape turns blue when it is sunny and pink when it is going to rain.

I presented this "barometer Mary" to Lúcia. She laughed, set it on her chest, and petted the fuzzy cape. I don't know what her laughter meant. I aspire to discovering what goes on inside her, but at the moment I'm glad I don't have the foggiest notion. Then I might feel guilty at giving up all efforts to file that article for my editor.

There's a big house that's a "halfway" home for ancient nuns, widows, and the like. I sleep there. I am in a strange country, but I lack better plans as to where to take myself. The fields stretch to nowhere, although there are cork trees with red branches and white medicine on their trunks so insects won't eat them alive. There are fig trees and sunflowers. The seeds get so heavy that the sunflowers stare at the ground. I shook one of them so that its face fell out. A widow named Teresa has offered to drive me in her car to a river nearby, the Mondego. I could go look at it, but I don't much see the point. I'd have to stare at it and act delighted, but inside I'd think, "Yes, that's a river," and I'd want to come back. This is probably the Londoner or the New Yorker in me.

In the pear tree behind the house, someone long ago (I have a theory, though I don't know why, that it is the person who threw out the pre-1975 backlog of letters) tied green bottles around pear blossoms. The pears grew whole inside the glass. When the wind blows, the bottles filled with their pears brush the leaves, and there's a music they make. I stand out there at night to listen. They are like voices.

When I looked at your name on your letter, a busybody nun reading over my shoulder kept pointing from your signature to the tree. I figured out that "Pereira" means "pear tree."

Lúcia stays in her room. Every day I take her for a walk in the garden, which is full of herbs, vegetables, and roses that I take pleasure in deadheading. She is bruised and heavy, as opposed to skeletal. She smiles a great deal, but it is a calm half-smile, not idiotic, and therefore I smile back. She is the Garbo we all carry within. She's fond of walnuts fried in cinnamon, and I cook it for her. It is not as ghastly as it sounds (meaning the dessert. I enjoy the frying-up).

Not everything is tranquil. An unfortunate contest is going on. The Mother Superior picks one person a night to watch by Lúcia's bedside. Now that Lúcia is nearing 100, there are rumblings that she may get a "last message." Jostling for this privilege is taking place. A 22-year-old Sister Ana is particularly vile in her eagerness. She stole a book from the Mother Superior's study and blamed it on Sister Margarida, who is what used to be referred to as "simple," and although Sister Margarida had scrubbed the chapel to earn the right to a turn with Lúcia, Sister Ana got the green light instead. I find this contest entirely morbid. When the night watch shows up, I exit. I pray that Sister Ana, or some other youngster desiring to get elevated out of the pack, sees Lúcia wave a hand that she should come closer, and when the young one bends near and whispers, "Yes? Yes?" that is when Lúcia replies hoarsely, "Your veil needs washing."

I am going on and on. I have taken a photograph of the Pear Bottle Tree and am enclosing it, with regards to you from a stranger.

Cordially,

Helen Dodd

April 20, 2000
Hayward, California

Dear Ms. Helen Dodd,

Your letter with the photo of the bottled pears arrived today, on my 45th birthday! It flew from you to me and the aim was true enough to enter flesh.

Wax body parts are burned as offerings. You buy a wax foot if you've hurt your foot, and when fire consumes it, your foot is (bah, humbug) healed. Entire wax dolls designate ill children, and though I wish they would leave me in peace, I see them when I shut my eyes.

You're correct about the meaning of my last name; I am back to it now that Ray has moved to an apartment up the road. We aren't divorced, but we're reduced to being "friends." I should rephrase that with the kindness he deserves: we're longtime friends, though it has been our unswerving tale to come and go without seeing much of one another. He gave me a pair of coral-colored sandals for my birthday.

(Yes, I read the official Vatican text this year of Lúcia's secret, which appeared in the major newspapers; it varies thoroughly in wording from one that was printed in a trashy magazine 15 years ago, though the sentiment—vague, fanged—is identical.)

Gina is my second daughter, born four years after that 1979 water-stained letter. She (like Ray) must work tonight; she tends orchids in a local nursery. The miracle will be if she graduates from high school, since she's refusing to take gym. I quarreled with Blanca, who's sneaking out and returning bedraggled at dawn; she screams that she's 21 and I can't boss her around.

Don't cry, Mami, said Gina. Her birthday present #1 was a package of sea monkeys. I realize they're only brine shrimp; you drop a frozen block into a tank and dozens of monkeys start swimming. Gina's gift #2 was a bolero vest, and bless her pointy little head, it's right on the cusp of what sterner types would call too young.

She served me lentil soup in a hollowed-out squash. She stuck candles in an angel cake from Safeway.

She cut a peach into wedges and floated them in water in our pitcher and said, "They're prawns." The tiny red legs fluttered, now that they were pulled loose from the stone.

Before Gina left for work I wore my new sandals and we played a CD of "Handel's Harp Concerto" and danced a box step, since neither of us dances well. I almost wept at how she clutched my hand; it startled me that no one has touched me that simply in ages.

I shouldn't have lapsed into a burst of energy when I was alone; while raking through my closet I found my cherry-colored skirt from high school. Drips & chevrons of red on white. My father bleeding over the porcelain of the bathtub. (I lost him like that when I was a child.) David on a stretcher with blood striping the sheet over him.

He was a breath-holder and promised he could navigate without the Chinese patrol spotting him. He could go whole minutes underwater, like the pearl divers.

Today in the grocery store I almost collapsed. I was selecting a papaya. They were old, with beads of sugar leeched onto the skin. Like the salt that stays on an ocean swimmer. Like the bead of fluid a man displays when he's ready to combust from waiting all day for you & the cover of night. Please don't think me crude.

David played the piano; he had a perfect ear. Once I risked us being caught by standing behind him and laying my hands on top of his, and the pieces, the songs, flooded out the taps of my fingers.

Helen: tapers were burning on my birthday table; I blew them out so that even small fires would be ended for you at least in one place on earth.

The pears in their bottles—like me in Hayward, pale face straining & hollering against the glass!—will be displayed on my bulletin board, next to the schedule at the Plunge (public pool), the Night Search for Owls Party at Sulfur Creek (sponsored by HARD, the Hayward Area Recreational District), and a flyer advertising the Portuguese Holy Ghost Festival. I am done with such religious pageants, but Gina assures me that she is designing the cape that will win the Grand Prize. She won't show it to me; it's a secret that she guarantees will astonish everyone. It can't help but move me, how she throws herself into a past she can't even define; I had to explain to

her that Luso-American means Portuguese-American because
Lusitania was the old Roman word for Portugal. I had to tell her
it is only half of who I am and therefore a quarter of who she is,
as if some quality of each of us is bound to recede.

But she could win the prize. I imagine its astonishing beauty,
her swallowed inside it.

I'll have to wait and see.

Your photo will stay pinned in view. But first I held it against
the bones of my chest. The house was empty No one was
watching. You will forgive me, I pretended I could inhale
the scent of a ripe pear stuck like a meat clapper in a bell of
a bottle, shaking out the tune of its growing. Its captivity. I
pressed it tighter and listened.

And then I didn't have to pretend any more.

I heard the music of which you spoke.

Yours,

Lara Pereira

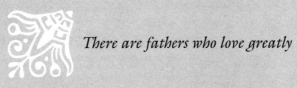 *There are fathers who love greatly*

Our Lady of the Artichokes

"We need to invent us a virgin," said my Tia Connie.

She came up with her scheme to fight the landlord while I was lying on the sofa muffled in its original plastic so that I crinkled every time I breathed. He had doubled our rent. She'd already remarked a dozen times, *May he die with his mouth twisted,* and I should have been fascinated that we were weeks from being thrown into the street, but all I wanted was for her to keep crocheting, watch her *Jeopardy* to learn better English (she also watched it in the hope that one night there'd be a category about the Azores and she could pretend to win thousands of dollars), and leave me to sharpening my fantasy that a banker (I'd named him Noland) would carry me away in his Jaguar. He was built like a cornstalk, with a tuft of yellow silk hair, and when I held him too fiercely, he'd say, *Ouch, you'll snap me in two.* Tia would be grateful for the checks we'd send. I'd write letters to her from Noland's greenhouse, among the irises. He'd share my passion for menthol cigarettes.

I sat up to make sure her plan was entering my ears right: we would issue a scream heavenward—it would ricochet back to earth—

that we'd beheld an apparition of the Virgin Mary outside this very apartment building—Estudillo Gardens—on East 14th Street in San Leandro. I asked why Mary would think of blazing a path here, and Tia Connie looked hurt and said, "I tend so nice those artichokes in the patch in front. She'll visit and be Our Lady of the Artichokes, perch on the thorns, and she'll cry and cry, then disappear. People will say, 'Come back to me, water me with your tears.' The landlord son of a bitch gets trampled, maybe to death. That part I cannot help."

The richly piquant part of this miracle was that I, Isabel Serpa, seventeen-year-old smoker, a roller of my eyes at Mass to convey that I believed nothing, would report the sighting; my infidel status gave me more credibility. Estudillo Gardens would be declared a shrine, and just try and lock out women and children where the Madonna had burned her outline in the exterior paint the shade of "sand dune," one of those timid California earth tones when mauve or chartreuse would be sunnier to come home to. Tia hadn't dreamt clear to the end of the story, but God could pick up the thread, seeing as He hadn't done much so far, but OK, He had all those baseball players crossing themselves, demanding the downfall of their millionaire enemies. I was beginning to suspect that all prayers were requests for immediate action, and no one was willing to sit inside any mystery—which seemed the point behind even a simple Our Father . . . a release of the will into a timeless thing I couldn't name.

"Don't be crazy," I said. "I'll get a job after school to help pay the rent."

"No! No! You save your energies, study, sneak cigarettes and talk big make-believe with friends, be a big saint or big cheese or somebody some day, my job is to worry, what the hell else do I have to do, answer me that."

"I've got worries, too."

"No, you no got you no worries. What you got now is a homework that you tell everyone Our Lady she talk with you."

She kissed the picture of Jesus in Gethsemane, snapped off the light illuminating him, and covered him with his brocade square, which she hand-brushed twice a week. She draped a baby's blanket over Senhor Zé, her canary the color of limes, before tucking me into bed under my crazy quilt my mother left behind when she ran off with a dentist from New Orleans, and I itched to burn the quilt and mix in sulfur and find out where she was hiding solely to mail the bitch the ashes, but Tia said that a crazy quilt was good for leeching madness out of your bones. My quilt she dry-cleaned whenever she sensed the cloth swollen, as if with a blue yeast, saturated with the panic and want and what-have-you that I failed to contain within me.

I heard Tia fitful in her room. Normally she was a goddess of sorts of equilibrium. Though she ate as she pleased, she was thin; she was fifty but her hair was pure black and she did not dye it. Her skin was perfect, soft as an eggplant, which is why once when I had acne boiling on my cheek, she dragged me to a lamp, pointed at my face, and said, What is that? as if she were a creature from another planet, and I yelled with shame and slapped her, but instead of hitting me back, she punched the lamp.

When I heard her slip out the front door, I put on my robe and snuck to the kitchen window to watch her waving around the pastry torch I'd given her for Christmas. Her family in Fontinhas had owned a bakery, and she liked blasting sugar into amber glass on the tops of puddings or wielding the fire to form hearts with arrows, or ribbons tied into bows with split, snake-tongued endings. She was using the torch to brand the outline of a veiled woman near the strip of garden at the front of our building, and my only prayer was that no one else was watching. The last thing we needed was a bill for repainting where a lady of bright light had burned, in toast colors, the nimbus of her body to announce the blank of her white heat.

I am not without my talents as a liar, and I own the raw stuff to have sounded the first note of hysteria—but I couldn't. Tia Connie had to enlist a chorus of widows. After her day's labor at Snow Drift, a Laundromat, she joined the prayer group kneeling with their rosary beads near the stain. The landlord must have figured it would create a bigger stir to have them hauled off for vandalism. My auntie's full name was Maria Conceição Amparo Serpa because she was born on the Feast of the Immaculate Conception, so the widows whispered that she and the Virgin were *just like this*—and they'd open two fingers into a wide scissors and then slam the scissors shut.

Clutching my schoolbooks, I walked past this display of the hardening that visits female solitude. The women were old frights, like the progeny of birds of prey and boulders; a guy's thing had rattled their privates for decades before dying, and it gave me a crawly feeling of pythons in crevices. Those penciled brows, hairs stiff enough to pry open locks, those wounded, glassy stares. I feared the widows would climb onto me in bed and suck my desires out through my eyeballs. *Blessed is the fruit of thy womb . . . blessed art thou amongst women.*

My friend Lily told people at school about the vigil, and I stared at my white shoes when Mark, the boy I liked, walked past. He always pretended I wasn't there. My shoes looked like lozenges of stale cream.

It was my youth that might have saved Tia and her friends from the howls of laughter: Old women! Biddies, *beatas,* here's-Christ-in-a-tortilla, sex-starved fools, the snickers barely containable in a two-inch column on page 10, Metro section of the *San Francisco Chronicle*. I waited for her reproach, but instead, at the dining-room table, under the framed picture of JFK festooned with a black ribbon—almost thirty years past his death—I heard her extending the rhythm of nonstop praying, *Oh, come to us. Oh, come to us.*

Late one night I caught her wrapping a noose of clothesline around the neck of her statue of Saint Anthony. "What's the poor guy done now, or is it me?" I said. If I found him head-down in the laundry basket, it warned me that I'd upset her and therefore he wasn't doing his job as the patron saint of love.

"Nothing, he does nothing, and I'm sick to death of nothing."

"You're not going to win him over if you hang him again," I said.

"He won't learn I mean business elsewise. I'll sew him a new cape if he behaves." "You're being gruesome, Titia." She held him up. "Isabel, Izzy. This is a statue. Not a man." "You never quit fighting with him. How's he supposed to like you?" "Well, OK, you and I always are fighting, too," she said, and dangled him by his neck in her clothes closet.

Smothered laughter brushed up and down us when we arrived at the Holy Ghost Festival. We were ten days from our eviction notice. I'd listened to Tia's chants of *Make my girl the next queen, please, Sant' Antão,* but this year the honor had been granted to Lúcia Texeira, a pretty girl with a bum leg. Her crown was like a wedding cake invisible except for its sparkling trim. I was assigned to traipse behind her, and I swear she was leaning on her cane and going extra slowly in an excess of piety and injury designed to make me a crazy woman, and so half by accident and half on purpose I kept stepping on her cape . . . and Lúcia countered with half turns and half smiles of forbearance, *Ah, yes, you live in those shitty apartments with the nut who sprayed her wall with a blowtorch,* and I lost my mind and kicked her in the back of the knee of her crippled leg.

Ten witnesses reported—to the police and to the Bishop—that they'd seen me kick Lúcia, who dropped her cane and flexed her stupid leg in both hands and screamed. And then—simply walked. The way everyone backed away from me I could have been a drop of acid.

Do not mess with the Holy Ghost, the faceless fire, Tia used to say. For Easter there's the eggs, Christmas we got the tree . . . what outward sign exists for Pentecost? In the early Church, doves were released in a basilica to provide a usable symbol, and they crapped on the heads of the faithful. Tia and I roared ourselves sick whenever she reveled in this story; "little dove" in Portuguese can also mean vagina.

I told anyone who'd listen that Lúcia liked infirmity, claimed it as a special mark, and I'd merely done what some doctor should have forced upon her long ago. Her kneecap needed realigning; I'd hap-

pily, freakishly reset her leg and ruined her act. But that night in front
of Estudillo Gardens, the old ladies were joined by mothers bringing
their children, and a few men, and I heightened the call in my brain for
Noland, my made-up boyfriend, to spirit me away. I fell into a chant
that filled the air of his Jag with a thorny calligraphy: *Save me. Save
me. Save me.* Then suddenly I was alone, wearing an apricot-colored
slip while standing at a window in Paris, with Noland due to arrive
and take me out—somewhere. He was off on international banking
business. He sat on sacks of silver coins, their metallic edges bulging
ridges in the cloth. We'd drink burgundy and eat little game birds
cooked with their bones. He'd show me where the knife should go
to cut them. When he finally entered our room I turned to him—
oh, the horns, cars, iron lace, melted-caramel light—and said, "I was
afraid you wouldn't come to me."

I heard a wail from the women outside calling for the Virgin, and
I summoned my courage; miracles do not come to those who wait,
God helps those who help themselves, etc., do not dream your life
away, etc., and I lit a cigarette and called Mark and exhaled smoke
when he answered. "We're awaiting our visitor from heaven," I said
sunnily. "Why don't you come by and watch with me?"

"You're as wacked as your father was," he said.

I stumbled outside, past the ladies. They didn't see me. I lived with
Tia across the way from a diner called Zinger's, with a revolving sign
of a chicken brandishing a revolver and wearing chaps and spurs. This
Great Chicken God of the West faced the outdoor cage of canaries
that Tia housed on the side of Estudillo Gardens. They were vivid and
tart-colored as jawbreakers, yellow, green, and orange, and one little
peach fellow who'd doom me to sobbing when he died, and one I'd
swear was blue and of a size that made him like a darting eye.

I walked to the movies so I could be alone in the dark. *Celine and
Julie Go Boating* was playing at the foreign-film place. Celine and Julie
dissolved a hard candy on their tongues and the sugar transported
them to a distant scene, where they solved a murder mystery. I'm not

sure how tears seeped through my head, but my scalp was sopping when the movie ended.

A light was shining in our kitchen. The crowd gazing at the stain of the Virgin had dwindled, but Zinger's was filled with the sheen of pilgrims, ions sparking other ions, metal filings in search of a magnet. I wasn't ready to face my aunt. I rested my head on my knees and cried for my father. He'd stumble home from the dairy, immaculate in his white uniform, and fall onto the couch with arms open, legs splayed as if broken, as if he'd been dropped from a height. White is rigor, white is melancholy. The method he chose was pills. An envelope addressed to me said: "Love is tender. Nothing is forever. Good-bye, my darling." He was especially proud of how well he'd learned English. My mother vanished. Conceição, his oldest sister, took me home with her. I was fourteen. That first night she cooked three pork chops and gave me two and a half of them while saying, We have us a deal, sugar pie, yes? You have a car, you take me where I need to go, here, there, store, church, Laundromat. I'll never go to the graveyard to visit my brother; he'll stay here now, some in your blood and some in mine."

The car she'd been referring to had been my father's, and I used to steal and drive it even though I was underage. Now it would be mine, until the DMV caught up with us. It was a Chevrolet with grillwork that gave it a frog's face. It grinned whenever it broke down on me. Tia named it "Mister Better Late Than Never."

The canary Senhor Zé was trilling like mad, and I walked in to find my aunt sprawled on the kitchen floor. "Jesus!" I said.

"Naw, only me, I polished the floor, thinking the people to see Our Lady will want to use the bathroom, drink a glass of water, my house needs cleaning, and I slipped. I take good care, bang, I get punished. Life. My neck is not so good."

I started screeching as I grabbed for the phone. "I'm calling an ambulance!"

"No! I am not a peasant! I have to change first into a good dress."

I told her to lie still, but she stood, her head tilted to one side. "I think maybe the floral one with the tie-bow because my neck, Isabel, my neck asks for a little cheering up."

The doctor said, "Mrs. Serpa? Are you aware that you've broken the bone the hangman tries to snap in the condemned?"

"Huh," she said, "so what."

She was fitted with a metal contraption to keep her head immobile for two weeks. Her skull was stuck in this silver birdcage of open slats with screws I had to tighten. I put her to bed and asked if it hurt. She said, "I'm alive. But what is wrong with my child?" I whispered I was fine, just worried sick about her. "Come here to me." I climbed next to her and curled up. With only one hand she could reach into my hair and form a loose braid. "What I know about boys is not so much, Izzy, but mostly it is air and attraction, and you cannot study how to make them want you." She said she'd been a lover of parties in her young days, but no one had dazzled her; she'd never slept with a man; it seemed that a girl must not pretend there's a dazzling when it's only hope churning a bit, or fear of loneliness churning a lot.

Like a comet forced into a chute, the world poured hard down our street and to our door, and my palm, on the door's inside, throbbed from the heat of the mob. Tia's surviving a broken neck was the second miracle. Even those who'd figured my kicking Lúcia resulted in a fluke cure were willing to rethink the violent, inexplicable ways of wonder. While I brought Tia her soup, sponge-bathed her, adjusted her metal cage, read her favorite tales from *A Thousand and One Nights,* we heard desperate believers tapping at our windows, groaning, all that heaving, sagging longing pawing at the stucco. The single-paned windows rattled in their casings, and noses and mouths left a smear of fog from their owners peering through the slit partings of the curtains to catch a sighting of the young saint and the old saint. Such tormented desire, such a willingness to whip and beat and shout the ordinary into sanctity. I would have laughed to the point of collapse if it hadn't been so scary. I no longer went to school.

I called Mark, thinking I'd ask what to do. I'd never been to his house, but I pictured it soothed with beige and lemon paints, with chrome that wore starbursts flung down from the track lighting. His mother would favor whimsical refrigerator magnets, strawberries with protruding seeds that would drive Tia and me to get up at night to pick at with our fingernails. Their cupboards would have cranberry waffle mixes, and Caribbean spice pouches, and stuffed green olives, and twisty metal with signature beads to wrap around your very own martini glass so no one would by mistake wash down what was yours. I howled in pain. "Mark!"

"What? Who is this?"

I hung up on him.

When I thought it was safe to sneak out to the grocery store, I was set upon with a shrieking that swallowed my own shrieking as hanks of my hair were ripped out by the follicles and my clothing got torn. Someone's nails gouged my bare breast.

A man pulled people off me and marched me to the door, but my eyes were shut tight and I only had the feel of his hands, which seemed to have the weight of wood, but pliable, on me, guiding me back home. When he'd delivered me to the door, waves surged against his back but he wasn't knocked aside, and when I opened my eyes and turned to say thank you, he was already on his way. He wore a blue uniform. His back was a large square, like the picture of a swimming pool. An orange bus waited at the curb.

I tried to joke with Tia that the third miracle was that I was able to get back inside owing to the kindness of a stranger. I'd observed that rivulets of blood now obscured the torch's stain, from people trying to scratch the shadow of the Virgin. On the television we saw the lame, the blind, the deformed, the arms with angry sores and the legs with ulcers, the women who'd pulverized their lifelines into raw meat from clutching rosary beads. Tia and I, starving, gnawed an ancient salami and stale Ritz crackers. Senhor Zé loosed an aria about being low on birdseed.

Our landlord—a single day before the notice was to have been posted—announced that he was a deeply moral man and, given the surprise events, he would postpone a rent hike. We listened to boots circling the house, stamping out a moat, and then—television was still our best way of fathoming what was going on right outside—the hawkers came, the vendors of Our Lady of Fátima and Guadalupe, the scapular-and-candle-waving brigade, the dealers in aromatic oils and talismans, the fortunetellers with card tables and the police scrambling to arrest them; not long after the bullhorns ordered everyone to disperse, a woman rammed her head against the thin membrane of Tia's bedroom window, broke it, got hoisted in, sliced her forehead on the cut glass, came staggering forth with red cataracts over her eyes, and shouted, "Kiss me," and Tia sat up in bed and said, "The truth is it was all my invention," but she blew a kiss in the direction of the bleeding woman. The people following the first invader through the window knocked the last fangs of glass out of the frame and ground it underfoot on the carpet so that no one else pouring in got injured, and from the inside of her metal halo Tia leaned forward to give each of them her best version of a kiss, saying, "The truth is it was all my invention, forgive me," and to a person they answered, "Please, I'm dying for your kiss," and into the night I directed the parade of strangers through the bedroom and out the front as if our apartment had turned into a stomach, and they asked the same of me, too, "Kiss me, dear, kick me if you like," and I'd offer my lips. My arms deepened to a midnight bruising from the grip of believers needing to touch me; my nose and half my face were abraded red. The flying glass had come to rest after being jagged little shears, pinking a touch the threads of the carpet.

I waited for the man in his blue uniform, but he did not show up for me to thank him right before I begged him to rescue us again.

Of course no third miracle occurred, and we were called charlatans.

The blood was fresh as new kill on the outside wall, and in place of the artichokes was a trench six feet deep, from everyone making souvenirs of the roots and any dirt that might have brushed against the roots and any second-degree dirt that had brushed against that dirt. My Chevy's frog snout was smashed, his hood dented, his feet stripped. Tia said, "My lips are a ring of fire from kissing that much, forgive me."

The taunts returned, and the landlord sent out a notice that in one month, per the previous plan, the rent would double, but out of the kindness of his soul he'd pay for a repainting and replanting—some zinnias? mums?—instead of bringing certain overwrought women and children up on charges.

Tia forced me to accompany her to a special bingo night at St. Joseph's in Alameda. Her metal headpiece had been removed and replaced with a cloth neck brace. My car wouldn't start, and she was frightened of traveling on the buses alone at night. The bingo ladies liked to carry bleach bottles they'd sawed in two, ringed with punch holes, and fitted with a drawstring knit top, like a purse, to carry their individual markers. "You can be so embarrassing," I said, refusing to carry it.

In the hall, with the other ladies with their bleach-bottle purses and the din of *N-17, O-42*, she made me help her cover the four cards she was working at once. "My luck she gotta change," she said. "Going to." "Huh?" "*Going* to change. You get in with all these Portuguese ladies, you start losing your English." "No, I do not." "Yes, you do, and as you recall, you keep asking me to bring such matters to your attention." A lady next to her shouted, "*Mexe!*" because the barker had taken a fifteen-second break. "Mexe!" yelled Tia. "See?" I said. "Oh, excuse me, I mean . . . *Mix!* Oh, my, that is a huge difference." "I should break your neck for real, Tia." "Go ahead, you do me a favor, I no have to live with you no more." "Let's go home." "I think you should buy a nice card, maybe win some money, fix your car, forget boys who they no good." "What boys? I can't get a date." "Because the boys they no good, otherwise they ask you out." "What do you know? You just keep me around for that stupid piece of shit car." "Yes, good, that is right. For your excellent car that is the reason we take the bus tonight." "I want to go home." "Aw, Madonna! I lose again!" She dumped her markers back into her bleach bottle; a new round began. "Are we going to be here all night, Tia?" "Until I win." "You've lost thirty dollars. This is a dumb way of paying the extra rent." "My luck she gonna change." "My luck is *going* to change." "I just say that." "Tia, please! Remember when you threw your back out working the slots in Vegas? I had to take you to the hospital then, too. I'm going to sign you up for Gamblers Anonymous." "I am not anonymous. Don't call me that. One time I pull one muscle in my back, you no let me forget nothing."

She was near tears when we left at midnight. She'd lost fifty dollars. We weren't speaking at the bus stop, except for me to hiss that it was likely we'd missed the last one of the night. The haze around the streetlights made it seem we'd been swimming in a heavily chlorinated pool for hours. "Aw, looka," she said. A bus picked us up. We were the only riders.

"Good evening, ladies," said the driver, and I stormed down the aisle to hurl myself into a seat, but she stood dropping the coins for our fares in the slot, one by one, chink, chink, chink, and I said, "Tia?" Because from the back, where I was, he looked like the man who'd ushered me home during the Our Lady of the Artichokes riot. "Sir?" I said. But he was staring at my aunt.

She said, "Where are you from, Senhor?" His name was Rui Alves, from Angra do Heroísmo, the capital city of the island of her birth. She adjusted her neck brace. He was driving a bus, he said, owing to his desire to be different, sort of a city fellow, not in the dairy business or on a ranch like the other Azorean men who came to California. He was strangely tall, with a rock-hewn face, black eyes; a widower, forty-eight. *A younger man,* said Tia. It came out like a breath.

"Hold on," he said, spinning the large round wheel pressed to his midsection. "You're that lady the Virgin she talk to."

"You were there," I said. "You showed up."

"I hadda go see, yes," he said. "It was big stuff on the news."

"And you saved me from the crowd," I said.

He turned around in his seat and grinned at me. "Naw," he said, "the Virgin she rescue you."

"The truth is she was a girl I dreamed her alive," said Tia. "The miracle, well—I invent her."

"I'm sure she's grateful you did that," he said. He seemed to switch between knowing English well and knowing it halfway.

She sat in one of the pews reserved for the infirmed, holding the silver pole and smiling at him while he drove. No one else boarded the bus; it was the last run until morning, and he knew right where to take us, if we were ready to call it a night.

They married a week later, and he moved into Estudillo Gardens with us and paid the rent.

While they were on their three-day honeymoon in Monterey, Mark appeared. He took my hand and said he'd never seen the genuine spot where that fuss had erupted about Mary and the vegetables, could I show him? He looked pale, but the bones in his face stuck out; it seemed to hurt him to have a skeleton bent on announcing itself every minute. The Zinger's chicken in its cowboy hat spun around, *bang*, spun around, *bang*. I led him to where the blood had been scrubbed off and the wall recoated. The burn mark was gone now, I said, as if he couldn't see for himself. We leaned there, and he kissed me. When I asked why this sudden change, why the interest, he said the caper I'd pulled with my aunt made me almost a famous person and famous people were hot.

"Almost—hot?" I said.

"Yeah."

"Then I need to tell you a story right now," I said. "Let's say you go over to that cage of·canaries and touch one. She'll lose her oils where your fingers went. The world gets in at those spots, and the canary dies."

"What are you going on about? You're famous but still crazy, I guess."

"It might be tonight or the next night or the next, but she won't survive. Haven't you ever learned that animals can flat-out die if someone touches them? In part they die of fright."

"Speak English."

"Go away, please. Please, before I change my mind."

Rui wasn't sure why I was moping, but he quickly had enough of it. One Saturday the three of us piled into my car and he drove us down the coast to the Mystery Spot near Santa Cruz, a point where a magnetic crossfire throws off everyone's balance. Balls roll up ramps. A person standing still seems to be tilting to the point of falling. A whisper disappears and pops out a corridor of air away. Water swirls in the wrong direction beneath a grove of redwoods, their stiff branches converting them into red candelabra. I held out my arms and my aunt and new father laughed and said I looked to be a mile off. At the point where the confluence was supposed to be strongest, Rui asked Tia, "What does it feel like?" Waves of her hair cupped gold from the afternoon ladling out reductions of its own light. She was wearing silver pumps like a runaway bride because beauty should cause a little pain. He'd started her on the habit of putting lanolin into gloves to wear at night after working all day at the Laundromat, and her veins had stopped bulging at the knuckles. She said something along the lines of it feeling like him, like somebody had changed him into an actual place, as far as she could see.

Tia got out her Singer machine at home. I hadn't known about her keenness for sewing. Rui came from a family of dairymen, but some of his neighbors back home had been fishermen, and as a boy he'd liked repairing the nets. He stitched on our missing buttons and instead of just tacking them on, he added the winding shank beneath, and he darned our socks, and one afternoon he and Tia outfitted the canaries in capes and bonnets. "Is Easter almost," she said. "They put on the new bird."

He took both of us to my senior prom at San Leandro High School and borrowed a bus from A.C. Transit; my car was in the shop again. With our orchid corsages we appeared like time travelers from the fifties at a party whose theme was "Punk Carnival," with glitter-clotted streamers from the ceiling of the gym to the floor. Rui found the music unbearable, so we each danced two waltzes with him and prepared for an early exit. He was good at weaving us clear of the gyrating bodies. He held my hand as if we were stepping even farther back, to the seventeenth century, as he said, left foot, right; good; now right, left. In the dark he dissolved, with that accent born close to my father's village, into lost male tones in waves breaking over the scene, the loud music, our silence: *Forget your heartbreak; put on your pretty dress; if you won't go to the party yourself, I'll take you, step here, now there, like this.*

He parked the bus on the grounds of the Dunsmir Estate, and we drank wine out of Dixie cups. I was thrilled that my blood might get tinged purple. Our faces were greasy from being up late. Tia had packed small round cheesecakes, and they were so pleasantly laced with the smell of diesel fumes that they tasted like travel.

Rui was with us for three years before he was diagnosed with leukemia. A fine white powder settled on his papery skin when he was finally in bed at home. Within his reach I propped a snapshot of him with Tia at the kitchen table, grinning; they'd just downed two glasses of buttermilk, the old live wires; and the drained insides were coated white, like the drippings caught off ghosts. The outdoor canaries were allowed in, uncaged; sometimes death will seize a tiny animal and leave a sick person in peace. But the birds were wily and flew so fast in the air of our rooms that they were beyond capturing, as if their bodies were melting, painting streaks in the air—lemon, orange, emerald, and a tartan crosshatch—and the colors solidified back into birds, and then again melted. The three of us were bound in the bright weave of these ribbons, and the birds pulled it tighter and tighter. "Put that tray down. Look at me," said Rui. I'd been fussing at his bedside. Death runs a scalpel through the gel surrounding us and says, Come out.

I sat down. I fell into his sights.

Good night, Father. Oh, what if prayer is really surrender? What if it is up to each of us to love in a way that gives birth into the dreamed-up realm of the world?

We did not mention that the notice had come that Estudillo Gardens was slated to be torn down to make way for luxury condos. Checks would be forthcoming as an aid to relocation for tenants. All of us would find it utterly impossible to buy even a closet in the deluxe new building.

Rui said he regretted that he would not hold the baby I'd have someday.

I laughed and took one of his hands in my own. "Baby!"

"Sure, just you wait and then you see," he said. Could we indulge him this once, he wondered, with a fantasy of him being a grandpa?

I might own a canary named Senhora Xica, in tones of marmalade, who screeches *joy joy joy* when I find out I'm to be a mother.

"Is it a girl? Or a boy?" said Rui, shutting his eyes.

"A girl," I said.

"And her name?" asked Tia, clutching Rui's other hand. Soon she would kiss his lips as the last moth rose from inside him; perhaps she'd want to swallow it so that she could follow him, but the moth would move at phantom speed and spiral into the air, to be eaten by the birds.

"Clara," I said. It means light, gap or opening, egg white, clarity. "She's stunning. She's dazzling."

"Clara!" shouted Tia Connie. "Beautiful! It's Portuguese and English! She'll be us from that other world, and you from this one! Heavens!"

"I send her my love," said Rui. "Teach her everything you know."

Come along now, Clara. Where shall we begin? This is how to eat an artichoke: cut off the thorns. The stem is called the leg, and it's an extension of the heart; don't throw it away. Toss the inner protective junk. The green pan of the heart is delicate; lots of work for small reward. Life is tender. There's a smile on you! A picture of you is burning through me forever. The leaves carry tips of the heart. Pull them hard between your teeth, my darling. Again. Again.

My Bones Here Are Waiting for Yours

Every year like clockwork, I stand by the Devils Postpile where my daughter lay buried under snow until the patrol found her body. She died seventeen years ago. I never pose in snow gear. I am always wearing my turquoise business suit and high heels; by trade I am a real estate agent. It is no longer available to me, the simple act of matching right time, right place, and right clothing. Or perhaps it is: I can be wearing my suit and showing a divorcée a boxcar of a house with its single rosebush, and distance vanishes and they're delivered to me where I stand: the basalt columns, the ice, the whiteness blotched with the failing of the sun. My name is Mary Smith. So ordinary that it suggests the exotic; I sound thought up by a forger, a fugitive.

My friend Lydia takes two photos—a close-up of me standing in front of the Devils Postpile and a long shot to show its height, with me as a smudge, reddish and blue-green, at its base. The turquoise against the whiteness is startling, a brightness in the shape of an hourglass. (My girl keeps me thin; I know that every year I must fit into that suit.) The heels of my shoes pierce like ice picks into the white body of the snow. My face and ungloved hands are scarlet with cold. The furious wind yanks my short brown hair. It was Lydia who sent enlargements of the first five years of these pictures to the San Francisco Museum of Modern Art, and now, as the seventeenth year passes, I take up half a wall with space reserved for many years more, so you see it is impossible for me to stop. The white space, unfilled, is a bit of unmarked snow in the city. I have great affection for it, and for my daughter's gift: being a famous photographer was once my heart's desire. She has given me something close to that, though it's Lydia's work, though I would gladly give back such a dream.

Critics have stopped saying, "This isn't art, it's accumulation," because the wrinkles carried over from being a grieving single mother (Years #1, #2, #3) have given way to vertical crevices. The frazzle-cracks deepen from Year #8 onward. I am draped in hard glints of light against folds of shadow. My blue eyes are specks of sky. Visitors to the display of "My Bones Join Yours in the Snow" never fail to note that by Year #11, my face is a replica of the Devils Postpile. I'm pleased that my body has become the map of my world. We cannot change our past fate, but we can intensify it. People are quiet and grateful as they gaze at the wall. They see that they are not alone with their secret fear that time does the opposite of healing.

My girl's name was—is—Delilah Smith. I had to wreathe such a common surname with a peace offering: *Delilah.* The lover and betrayer of giants. She's like a wildflower that's a blazing pink on the burning hot or burning cold of the desert's floor.

But this year everything has changed. Seventeen years old when she died, seventeen years gone, the balance from now on weighing more heavily toward death, Delilah has decided to act like a teenager and wild child and star. She had been wearing her charm bracelet when she died—what were you thinking, you little fool?—and the cold cracked it open and scattered the pieces. Four items were not recovered: the tiny crescent moon, the miniature whale, the Scotty dog, and the microscopic ballet shoe. But last week, a miracle, a skier found the Scotty dog near Warming Hut II on Mammoth Mountain, miles away. She had mentioned wanting to love an animal without having to care for it, so I gave her that as a joke. Her tenth birthday. It must have traveled through the inside of a bird.

I seldom visit the exhibit, but Lydia reports that lately there are murmurs. People are no longer satisfied with my predictable slide into stone. One woman said, "I need Mary Smith to fall in love."

When will she tell us there are reversals to keep us alive?

When will she let us say, "Look at her glowing face! She's been adored and ravished, torn limb from limb"?

And I heard Delilah's own voice. After her father and I divorced, her favorite project was trying to fix me up. *You've milked the daylights out of grief, Mother. Now how about the grief of a real live romance?*

I announced a reward for the return of the missing three items. "Whale & Moon & a Girl's Love of Dance," said a headline in the *San Francisco Chronicle*. One thousand dollars for each one put back into my grasp. How active the dead really are. They don't so much fling memories at us, or warnings to seize the time; they set contests in motion, actions born of excitement, and how beside myself I am to be informed that when I am dead I will still want to know what happens next. Let the treasure hunt begin, let Delilah order up a search for gold in the hills, the never-ending story of California, let me secure the last of her, let me please put my bones against living ones, let a man hold onto me without my scaring him because it is so frightening when a woman screams for help in pulling off her winding sheet.

I believe it is carried somewhere on the air, Delilah telling me what happened. I would like to solve the mystery of why she drove east and then south on the 395 toward the Mammoth Valley rather than north from the Bay Area to Eureka, where she was supposed to stay with her boyfriend, Christopher Rosetti, and his parents at their cabin. She was supposed to join Coach Bellevue and the rest of the swimming team at Mammoth the following week. Delilah should have been alert to matters of precision. She was a backstroke expert and knew how to sink her head to shave off microseconds and how to touch out an opponent at the finish. A fearful part of me wants to learn if she was still alive and immobile in that snowbank when a coyote or bear chewed off her right hand. The public leaves this delicately unsaid, that the bones of her right hand have vanished, that my getting back those missing charms will be the closest I can come to recovering her full remains. She'll kill me yet, my wayward girl.

I will be left to guess how her eyes painted the black of the night and the white of the snow. Delilah was a synesthete. I took her to a special doctor for tests. She got written about in a national magazine; even as a child she was hungry for public attention. I first noticed her synesthesia when I helped her write an essay in third grade. I wrote G-L-A-S-S, and she said, "Red with spots, white, something like those bugs that live under bricks, pink, pink." She told me she saw colors when people spoke. They spilled from everyone's mouths and ran together like the Cosmic Circus that Daddy made, drops of food coloring on a plate hit with blasts of dish-washing liquid that made them dance around and mix into purple and orange. I told her to drink her milk, and she cried, *I can't, it's a blue noise so how do people swallow it?* Her senses were knotted in a ganglion inside her, and the strings of her nerves flowed to the ends of her body, to her fingertips, nose, ears, eyes, and skin, in a jumble. This was a girl who might have solved the riddle of the color and sound of being in love, if she had only gotten that far. She was eight when I played the piano and she sat back with her eyes closed in a way that made me ask, "Sweetheart? Does it look like something, the sound?"

It's saying, *Lion, lion, Momma.* Some lions were roaring in the living room and it was hard to see straight, what with their noise like paintbrushes covering everything with the red of their tongues.

I wondered if she had invented this to unnerve me, but the doctor testing her spoken words and she spelled them in colors, and a year later he asked her the same words, and she described them with the same shades. Synesthetes usually have their own codes, but no one, he said, can remember everything; the fakers get tripped up. She scored ninety-eight on the test. Delilah would have traveled the world and understood everything, and who could possibly bear such a deluge? In the article in *Time* her picture has the caption, "Delilah Smith of San Leandro, California, Is a Matisse of the Invisible." She is sitting near Dr. Jake O'Grady; her dark blond hair is held in place with a crimson headband, but a front tooth is missing because it was loose and she got impatient and tied one end of thread around her tooth and the other to a doorknob and then slammed the door. "What color was that, Lilah?" I asked. I meant the pain, the act, her shout. I was serious, but she figured I was trying to catch her in a lie.

I can't help you with that, Momma. She glared at me, looking wounded. *Some things don't do anything but hurt.*

I was distraught. She thought I was like everyone else, making fun of her. *(What color is the spit I'm spitting at you, Matisse?)* I spent a day with a migraine, looking at those discs that explode in the air. I gave her the moon for her charm bracelet, in a box under her pillow, with a note that said, "The moon is white, and white is the part of the spectrum that contains all colors. The night is dark, because it contains them all, too. You are a girl who will go farther than the moon. I am sorry—Momma."

The ballet shoe is from her father, Tobias Smith. He danced with her head on his shoulder, her arms around his neck, her feet dangling. He sang, *Why, why, why Delilah/My, my, my Delilah* while she got helpless laughing. The letters in "why" startled her, since they gave off sparks and apparently ran together as gold. We had a lemon tree in our yard with so much fruit that they got as swollen as grapefruits before we used them, stretching their insides until they had no flavor. When Toby was home from work—he was a traveling salesman for a fabric manufacturer—we sat at a card table in the yard and drank water with sugar and mint leaves that I had cleaned with a paper towel, and we said, "Oh, really, Madame? Oh, is that so, fine Sir?" We liked each other very much. When I still wanted to be a photographer, I took many pictures of us below the tree with its yellow globes. On some of those lemons the nipples were bigger than mine, and one year the trunk got split by lightning so it gaped open at the fork, and I could never go past it without a blueness I could not name.

When Tobias came home one day from his travels and kept vomiting, with me holding his forehead, his brown eyes watery and his hair with the silver spilling out from the temples, I said, "Tobias? Have you fallen in love?" On account of my daughter I was learning to decipher the air. How could I not read the brightness off his skin, how could I not be happy for a friend with such great fortune? I had married him after a love affair of mine, when I imagined all of that was done for me, the wildness and longing, and I had found someone with whom I could curl up and go gently to sleep.

Delilah seemed happy for him, too, going to see him and his new wife and a new daughter, Andrea, in Michigan every summer and for Christmas. She said her father still liked funny dances. At holiday time, while clearing snow from the driveway, he twirled the shovel like a rifle, doing a this-shoulder-to-that-shoulder routine from a military parade, while Delilah and Rebecca, the new wife, holding the baby, laughed behind the glass. The lights decorating their eaves were thin icicles, those ones like pretty, white versions of nerves. His book of fabric samples would sit open on a counter when he was home from his travels, like a thick Bible written entirely in Delilah's language. *Rebecca talks in reds and blacks*, came the report, *like lions*, and that pleased both Delilah and me no end, to think of Tobias with someone who spoke with vivid edges, and that when he unfurled his bolts of cloth, stamped with autumn leaves or ribbed with emerald thread, they cascaded down from tables and were like so much tinted water, now that he had gone into another realm.

Delilah wanted me to be as happy as Tobias, and even then it felt truly for me and not out of any wish of hers for a new parent. She would put too much purple eye shadow on me when I had a date, and I would wipe off half the rouge in the man's car. I'd open my purse and find her notes, *Smile! Men really like that!* Written in bold blood-red on snow-white paper. What did my fourteen-year-old girl know about any of that? But I needed her coaching and her plots, me running into her math teacher by accident, her ordering me to one of her swimming meets when Peter Roseland's divorced father was going to show up. I loved her, though not the men. The man before Tobias made desire rip holes in my skin, and of course when you're porous like that the world flows in and pretty soon that's the end of it, you're everywhere and everything and no longer yourself. I loved him more than anyone before or since. I cannot say his name because the letters of it go like razors into my skin. In our three years together I never asked him to leave his wife, because if he had to think too long if he wanted the one or the other of us, then I did not want him, and yet I also believed it proved how much he wanted me, for him to be careful about coming to me when he could make it last. But all of that happened a sensationally long time ago.

They found the whale!

A young couple on a trek half a mile from the Devils Postpile found the whale!

The television cameras were at my house as I wrote the young man and young woman their thousand-dollar check. They had wide smiles on their snow-burned faces, what Lilah called "gash in the fire." They tried to be patient as I showed them pictures of Delilah, the framed one from *Time.* I said that it was a pity that when she turned into a teenager she started to lose the ability to see the shapes of sounds; they stared at me and wanted to leave.

Ashamed, alone, I watched the news report of me handing over money to the lucky couple, and in a dizzying splice the station followed this with the original newsreel from the year Delilah's body was found. We look so young, so capable of absorbing a jolt of fresh shock: me, bracing myself in the door jamb; her swimming coach, Mr. Bellevue, already up at Mammoth with his family and saying, "It was next week she was supposed to come here. With the rest of the swimming team. It's our annual holiday in the snow, because snow is after all just another form of water." His eyes have the wetness of clean diamonds. I get to see them again, Lilah's best friends, Joyce and Elaine, sobbing, their hands with pointed blue fingernails over their faces. Joyce, a fellow swimmer, a freestyler, has grown heavy out in the country, where she breeds Alsatians. Christopher, the boyfriend, is in tears, saying, "We waited, I waited and waited . . . " Christopher is married now and has three children, and he makes an annual pilgrimage from Monterey to the museum to see the new photos, to take me to lunch with his family and say, "You must move on, Mrs. Smith." He still calls me Mrs. Smith. I look at his well-behaved children and quiet, pleasant wife, and I cannot understand why my daughter did not drive to Eureka to meet this fellow and his parents, if her crossed nerves finally did something to cross her wrong with time-telling; maybe she thought, Mr. Bellevue is already in Mammoth so I'm due there. Me, Mr. Bellevue, Joyce, Elaine, Christopher: the film is sepia now, going into the honey tones of age in the old canister at the television station and taking us along right with it, one coat of dissolve for each passing year.

And doesn't one thing, even dead and boxed, always lead to another? I saw David Heathrow, the reporter, first at a distance and then getting closer, coming up the walkway to my home, and the glare of the sun sent out a palette knife to scrape off bits and pieces of him, taking them into the light so that he was in the air and I could breathe him in. His hair was black, and I was so very young when I learned from Lilah that you should not be afraid to fall into blackness because it contains all shades, everything. Someone at *Time* must have watched the news about the unearthed whale and said, Let's do a reprise, we covered the girl once and now let's cover the mother. They sent me David Heathrow, but I was thinking, *Wicked girl. Wicked girl.* Naturally it was Delilah sending him to me.

His eyes were blue like mine, but that does not mean I felt I was looking into myself, it meant confirming that parts of me resided separately in others and parts of them were in me. The hairs on David's chest and around his penis were also black, and white, and I cried over that—leaking out of his body was everything precious and nonprecious and the roots boiling out of the invisible chemicals inside men. I cried so much over the wonder of that. He said, "There, there, shh, don't let me hurt you." But it does hurt, not to touch a man for over ten years and suddenly you're worse than laughable, you're a fifty-six-year-old woman who's cracking open. I cannot recommend it unless you can live twice. Once to marvel: the instant he put his hand between my legs I rose with a screech off my bed, and he remarked, "You're like no one else, darling." Once so you can feel what it's like, to crack off layers like mica sheets and then further ones, past the time you're sure you've run out of them, until you're in a panic that if he puts his tongue into your mouth one more time it will be the hammer at the right angle to send the whole frozen fucking statue of you into rubble. If only you could have another life after that: never to suffer through such a drought. David Heathrow was fifty, divorced, very tall, and he stayed in bed with me long enough so that I forgot the time, until one day when we were both naked together and I was lying on my stomach and he breathed into my ear, "I love it this way" and entered me from behind, and I reared up and twisted around to kiss him, wanting the front of myself plastered to him right as my back was pressed to him, the wetness pouring down my thighs to paint my insides onto him. Such small, small cascades and drops were flying out from the seal of us. I wanted him to take front, back, and the water of me with him when he left, because that was when I knew he would leave.

He said, "I love it this way," to enter a women who's on her stomach, right as I was going to say, "I love you, David." A simple typical story: the man says I love it, and the woman says I love you. She thinks of saying, "I want to know the things that you could only learn about yourself by being with me," but he goes away. He came in the air and to the air he returns, and how could I not love the vanished man for as long as I breathe, the joy of him, since the stone over me got chiseled and then knocked aside so that I could crawl out, though now there's only a tiny, tiny pink curl of me. Whatever will I look like next year, the hourglass shape of myself swallowed inside my turquoise suit at the Devils Postpile? Why, all I need is a hook through the soft, opalescent peak of my tiny scalp, and you could latch me onto a charm bracelet and I could ride with you and without your seeing it I could hug onto your pulse and that would be enough to make me come, and keep coming, from the throb of the life in you.

But the air shocked me, shriveled and raw like that, and the sun liquefied my edges until I imagined my eyelash-sized bones would poke through. Lilah did not see pain as a color, though some synesthetes do; I wondered what it meant that everything about me after David seemed lodged on a band of yellow. I would show houses and earn my living and then escape, ashamed because these clear fluids were still leaking out of me, and I thought the layers were done cracking open but they kept at it and at it and I was still shedding them as I took a racing jump into the swimming pool. "Snow is another form of water," said Coach Bellevue; in water my bones get to swim along with the bones of my daughter in the snow. A woman is such a runny thing even when she's good and whole. I never asked my daughter: *What color is the water when you swim? Since you're a backstroker, Lilah, is it blue of sky, yellow on water? Red from the sun? Or is it nothing at all? When you put your face in and play that childish game of saying: I've hid my face and so now I am invisible!—does that have a shape? Does clearness count, does the blur of being in water have a scent?* There is so much I still need to learn. Tell me why you drove to Mammoth a week before you were supposed to be there and left your car and trooped past the "Road Impassable" sign, and why you lay down in a storm and lost the bones of your hand to the animals. The coach was there with his family but the team was supposed to follow in a week and you were supposed to meet Christopher and then go to Mammoth on your way back home. You're all mixed up.

I get things backward, too, dear. I could tell you that I gave up being a photographer when I understood that I lacked perfect focus. My eyes failed. As a child I would go to Dr. Palmberg, a nice man who held out a photo of a fly where the wings had the illusion of standing straight up, and I would hold my fingers inches from the wings and say, "But why aren't I feeling them? Aren't I touching them?" He would give me drops to dilate my eyes, and I wore flimsy dark glasses with cardboard earpieces and even my best friend, Maggie, made fun of me: "Where's your cup? Shouldn't blind people have cups and pencils and say, 'Who will help me?'" It is our friends who surprise us with their cruelty, but general kindness is unfailing because it is always a reaction at large to any hint of death; that's why the visitors to the museum are cheering me on.

It's not a color but a dazzling, the water when I swim in it. Now that I'm this tiny my heart has shrunk to a cherrystone. Think infinitesimal, and you will attract infinity.

I lift arms, pull, kick feet; touch wall, turn, go back and do it again.

Delilah was thirteen when she went with me on a photography trip, a seminar with a dozen others to the Alentejo, the interior province of Portugal. The cork trees peeled back their bark on some of their forking branches, and Delilah said they were women opening their legs and taking off their stockings in the warm air. The rest of the trees were red, and the clay ground was slit up even redder. We ate goat! The sauce was made of onions, flour, carrots, and the animal's blood. We went to the Chapel of Bones. Ex-votos of hair hung on the wall: *I give you a part of my body, please, God, give me the love I request.*

One woman fainted, and Delilah fanned her. We learned that the femurs, skulls, arm bones—I wish I could name by science all the pieces we contain—that formed the chapel were from the bodies of monks cleared out of the graveyards to make room in a small coun-try for the next wave of the dead. *Nos Ossos Que Aqui Estamos Pelos Vossos Esperamos* said the legend over the door: Our Bones Here Are Waiting for Yours.

Delilah whispered: I can hear the skulls, Momma, because of all the *shh, shh* sounds the living language here makes, they're echoing

it, but in gray that opens into whiteness. The gray and white aren't so bad, they're like lots of colors, only faded, or wet, I don't know.

Hanging on the wall was the corpse of a man who would not disintegrate properly. We were told this was terrible, like a curse. He was that color that lemon juice makes if you write with it and then

NOS OSSOS QVE AQVI ESTAMOS PELOS VOSSOS ESPERAMOS

hold a lit match below the paper, not enough to burn everything to ashes but close enough to make the invisible writing appear, a burnt sienna, reddish brown. It's all mixed up, said Delilah. The femurs are long but the shape of their color is "O," and the skulls are round but say "Shh." One of the few absolutes on which synesthetes agree is that "O" tends toward whiteness. She said, loudly, that she would never understand why it was a curse for the man's dead body not to disintegrate, that she would want the same thing. An American nun in our tour group said, "Shh!" And then to me: "It means the soul of that man is not at rest."

Delilah said to the nun, "That dead body had a secret love. That makes him like the earth and he doesn't want to leave it."

"May I ask how you can guess such a thing?" said the nun.

"That is *so* easy," said Delilah, rolling her green eyes. "A secret love is always the answer."

I hit the wall of the pool, and my bloodied lip puts a red ink like a blot of a tiny mouth into the water. David once bit my lip and said, I'm so sorry, but I said, Oh, no, I'm happy to have you draw blood; I figured I had none left.

I dress and run a comb through my hair, and with it still wet I drive to Mr. Bellevue's house. It's Spanish style, with a terra-cotta roof that catches pine needles and an iron railing around a red porch. When he answers the doorbell a toddler comes up and grabs his leg. Mr. Bellevue has a swimmer's thick chest, and I can almost picture it, Delilah's long blond hair in a fan over that hard flesh. He was at Mammoth the week before the team was due. He was with his family but Delilah showed up, and they had the talk about nothing lasting forever, and off she trooped to lie down in the ice.

The voice of his unseen wife says, "Who is it, dear? Who is it?"

I take the whale out of my purse and whisper, "Will you keep this to remember her? It's a water creature, and it makes sense for you to have it."

His eyes are shot with purple, with stars, with fear, even though he sees I'm not there to accuse, to confront. Until right then I wasn't sure I knew the truth, but now I am.

I will not leave until he takes this microscopic whale like a bullet that will explode his brain open into a million infinite pictures of her.

I put it in his hand and close his fist around it.

His wife, slight and with copper hair, arrives and says, "Mrs. Smith? Are you all right?"

I could say, Water and pleasure, bones and their secrets. Look at how the dead speak, look at how the living cannot speak.

I only want him to hold onto the pictures he carries inside himself like part of his skeleton, of my daughter desperately kissing him, of him running his hands down her back as they stand in the coaches' office while her boyfriend, Christopher, the devoted soul, the boy ready to carry her over a lifetime of floodwaters, the boy she can't bear hurting, the dull future, sits waiting with his family in a cabin. And she can't bear it. She must throw herself into the waters that will carry her under.

"Good-bye, Mr. Bellevue," I say. "Good-bye, Mrs. Bellevue."

The ballet shoe and the moon remain out there. The bones of Delilah's hand—still out there. This year Lydia and I went to New York, and I bought an aqua shift. She took two pictures of me wearing it in front of the Empire State Building. One of me up close and the other to show me as a smudge against this manmade tower. The visitors to the museum will say, Mary Smith remains in sorrow, but it is the sorrow of a woman who is boundless.

Could my daughter have been pregnant by Coach Bellevue? Could that have been the reason for her despair? My grandchild like me, a pink curl of a minnow, no bigger than a charm.

I'll never know. This little fish would be sunk into the ground. I can only know that Delilah's hand awaits mine. Better that the flesh never dissolve, better that the bones swim in the earth. What is it called? Flesh incorruptible. Giving off the odor of violets that's said to signal sanctity. In death we start out red as the river of hearts knifed open. That can be my last entry on the long, long wall: tack up my corpse holding a replica of my Delilah's naked hand, the two of us refusing to break down, bodies without end. Call us incorruptible; call us never at rest.

The Man Who Was Made of Netting

Manny Cruz bought his daughter a cape that would stun everyone into silence. It cost him ten thousand dollars, half of which he had taken from the Miscellaneous account at his brother-in-law's furniture company, where Manny kept the books. He had been writing himself one-hundred-dollar checks every week for a year, and Frank, his brother-in-law, had not noticed. The petty-cash fund was large. Besides, Frank was busy spending several hundred every week taking clients to lunch. Manny planned to replace the money as soon as humanly possible.

Whenever he saw his daughter, Gemma, huddled in her room, what he had done felt splendid; this time luck would not fail him. A Hollywood scout—a cousin of a friend of a friend, something like that—had heard that dozens of girls in amazing capes turned out every spring for the Portuguese Holy Ghost Festival in Monterey, and he was coming to have a look. The festival's organizer, Maria Duarte, was told that a movie was in the works about a miracle striking a girl in a procession. She was supposed to levitate or get the stigmata; stories about spiritual calamities were popular now. Some producer must have

said, Hey, we'll make it Portuguese, they already have those parades
and the costumes are great, and we haven't touched those people
since *Mystic Pizza,* and that one made Julia Roberts a star.

All of this was fine with Manny—Gemma's cape was going to
catch the eye of the scout. Every family was in an uproar about this
Hollywood lottery, but Manny was calmly assured about winning.

The night before the festival he did not sleep well, and when he
rushed to his daughter's room in the morning he was surprised to
find her still in bed. Her cape, sheathed in plastic, was hanging on
the outside of the door of her wardrobe. "Gemma?" he said. "Time
to get ready. Aren't you excited?"

She turned over in bed, a sullen, leaden mass, and ignored him. Where
had his child gone? When was it exactly that she had left him?

"Gemma?" he said. "Your cousin is probably already waiting for
us downtown."

"Oh, God, leave me alone," she said.

He had been there at the first scan of her: on the sonogram she
began as nothing but a white spiral with a feathering attached. Already
that was her, real, a mysterious coil, clashing with his idea of her. When
Manny was a child his mother had pointed to a pregnant woman and
said, "She's taking the time to knit her baby's bones together," and
even when he was married at eighteen and about to be a father, that
image stayed with him. He pictured knitting needles clicking some
cells into a spine, then ribs, and then came the glomming on of more
cells that knew how to knit up a person with a spleen and nipples and
a predisposition. He loved the soft down that made a seam on the
back of his daughter's neck, and everybody else's as well—that was an
inspired brushstroke of creation that had blessedly, finally, nothing to
do with any function and everything to do with arousing compassion,
especially when you saw it on a person who was sleeping.

He went into the bathroom to dampen a towel to wash her face.
The towels were so old that the flowers and fruits on them appeared
to have been held up against flowers and fruits so real and potent

that they had bled faint impressions onto cloth. When Manny's wife had run off years ago with a rich, older man, she had said, *Everyone is replaceable, Manny. Everything and everyone.* He found her parting comment so vile that he held onto things—clothing and linens, pots and pans, plants—until they disintegrated.

He found Gemma up and encased in sweat clothes, sunk heavily on the end of her bed. Her dark brown hair looked as if she had combed it with knives. "Daddy," she said, "would you do my hair in a French braid?"

He had no skill with beauty. He did not know any of the terms. "What's that?" he asked.

"Grandpa knew," she said. "What's your problem?"

"I don't have a problem, Gemma," he said. "I'm in a good mood. Why are you wearing those clothes? Get into your gown." He handed her the towel and told her to scrub her face. Other parents were calling in hair stylists and makeup artists and were generally going mad because of this scout. He should have planned for some help like that. Another mistake—part of his lacking any talent in matters of grace. Gemma was seventeen but looked like an unhappy, fat thirty-year-old. He would control his temper and cheer her up, or all the money and art on earth that she might carry on a cape would not win her to anyone.

"Show me how to do a French braid," said Manny. "If Dad learned, I bet I could."

"Oh, forget it. Christ."

"Christ got busy and sent me instead." Manny didn't blame Gemma for missing his dead father; he wanted him back, too. She had lived with her grandpa during the years when Manny's gambling was bad, but that was over now. He'd made a vow to her to quit.

When Gemma had on her silk white empire dress and high heels, Manny took the wrapping off the cape, and even Gemma stared at it for a minute and could say nothing. It was changeable fabric, the kind that had a warp that was one pattern and color and a weft that was another. The cape had a lengthwise gold weave with rusts and reds that looked like tongues of fire, and the opposite weave was brilliant white. On the whole sweep of it sequined doves held ribbons attached to fishes in a sea that was a froth of lace. He had gone to Palmira Flores, who lived in Merced and did nothing but make Holy Ghost capes, and he had said, "It has to be better than anything you've ever done." After she'd huffed and said that everything was her best, he'd said, Make this more than everything. He handed over his ten thousand dollars, and she opened the lids of bins and crates, and the room gleamed as if the tide had drawn back from a wreckage of treasure chests, rubies draped here and there, braids, laces—he did not have the vocabulary to describe these things. Palmira Flores needed to teach him the terms "empire dress" and "changeable fabric."

He took the cape off its hanger, and the slats of light through Gemma's blinds changed it from white to red, then white to rust, as if it were a living thing, and the fishes' eyes sparkled and so did the eyes of the birds that were meant to be the Holy Ghost, and he put it on her and tied the gold ribbons that looped down over her heart.

"This weighs a ton, Daddy," said Gemma.

"You know the saying 'Beauty knows no pain'?"

"No."

"How about the French saying 'One must suffer to be beautiful'?"

"We aren't French."

He helped her gather up the long train so that they could drive to the plaza in Old Town near the Bay. Manny wished that the waterfront could look less tarted up and more like what it used to be, the place of Steinbeck, with wonder or some shock of actual life seeped into everything, including the rickety wharf. He and Gemma lived inland. His sister, Glória, was married to Frank Silva, Manny's boss, and they lived with their daughter, Daisy, in their house on a bluff.

He held out his hand to help Gemma step from the car. Queens and their attendants, in capes and crowns, milled around, sequins flying and parents shouting and trains being spread out with their plastic underliners to protect against the ground. The brick plaza was lit up with violent color, flowers, screams, biers with Our Lady of Fátima or Saint Anthony and the Paraclete doves, and paper and tin ornaments waving in the damp, salted breeze; baroque overload— all good, all just right; Pentecost was the feast when the Holy Ghost appeared as tongues of fire over the heads of the apostles, huddled frightened in a room. Suddenly the apostles caught on fire and burst out into the world.

And now here was Gemma, out of her room on a bright Sunday. He unfurled his daughter's train, and a little girl stopped to stare. She said, "Oh, you must be the main queen."

"Not the main one," said Gemma, and she smiled. "I'm one of the queens today, though."

Manny could feel the stirring in the air, the last-minute fussing and glances over the shoulder, an air of: Where is he? Where is our special guest, the star-maker? He recognized the Dutras, the Batistas, the Bettencourts, and Amélia Pavão, a rich girl. He couldn't help it; he needed to survey the competition. He guessed that Amélia's cape also cost about ten thousand dollars—the wealthy families paid from two to five thousand to eight or ten thousand. Girls like Clara Medeiros wore borrowed ones. Amélia's gown was lovely, but Gemma's was stunning. People were studying it in awed silence, and he felt relief and a sudden blaze of confidence.

"Here comes Daisy," Gemma said.

Manny's niece ran to them and threw her arms around Gemma and said, "Your majesty!" The girls giggled. Daisy's cape was elegant but plain, red silk with jewels on the perimeter and a short train.

"Where's the Hollywood guy, Uncle Manny?" said Daisy. "Everyone's trying to guess who he is."

"Oh—" he tried to sound as if he had forgotten about the scout. "I think he's going to show up at mealtime."

"When we're picking meat out of our teeth?"

"That's what I've heard," said Manny. He adored his niece as much as he disliked working for her father. She was generous in her attention to Gemma. There was a lightness about Daisy that was not weightlessness but a grip on the power of light. She played the flute and knew jazz dancing and was on the speech team at Monterey High, and although she wasn't a knockout, with her wide face, high forehead, and large teeth, she had a way of opening up those huge features and enjoying herself. Manny was made aware, as he looked at her cape, that this was another kind of beauty, the kind that knew what it was and therefore, being essential, did not have to try too hard.

Daisy's parents emerged from the crowd. Frank required a wide berth and walked heavily in his boots. Glória's face was drawn. At some point Manny had lost his sister, too. When had that occurred? When she married Frank? She was plastered with makeup and wore wheel-shaped earrings that struck him as aggressive.

"Uh oh," said Daisy. "Here comes the wrecking crew."

Frank arrived and shook Manny's hand, then he kissed Gemma's cheek and began studying her cape. "Nice," he said, looking at Manny. "Very nice."

"Hello, Manny," said Glória, and closed her eyes and screwed up her face to kiss the air near him.

"You haven't been to Artichoke Joe's for a round of blackjack, have you, Manuel?" said Frank.

"Shush, Frank," said Glória.

Manny kept his breathing even, but heat glowed out of his skin. He should have known that Frank would wonder where he had gotten the money for a cape like this.

"No," said Manny, "that part of my life is over. You know that. I promised my girl."

Frank shrugged. "A joke, Man-well."

The procession lined up, with teenagers holding banners—Luso-American Sports Club, Knights of Columbus, Monterey IDES, *Irmandade do Divino Espírito Santo,* the Brotherhood of the Holy

Ghost. Queens, senior and junior, were here from Monterey, the Bay Area, and the valley towns, with attendants who held onto the loops stitched into either side of every cape so that it could be held out on display at its grandest width.

"Time to go!" said Daisy.

Frank and Glória went to join the procession, but Manny decided to stay on the sidelines to keep Gemma from being nervous. He leaned over to kiss her and whispered in her ear, "Go knock everyone dead."

It would all have been worth it, even if Frank caught him, even if he couldn't get the money back into the books in time: all worth it. Because people stood aside and inhaled sharply as if they were having trouble breathing when two girls took the side loops and fanned out Gemma's cape. He heard sighs and "Ooh" and "Oh, heavens" and "God," as if everyone were making love to someone invisible. Gemma's face brightened and opened as she stepped behind the Monterey banner, and right then she was lovely, too.

"Daddy!" she called out. And she didn't say, "Thanks, Dad," but that was all right. That was all right. She said, "Wouldn't Grandpa love to see me now?"

He said, and hoped it was loud enough for her to hear over the din, "I'm sure he's seeing you, darling."

Manny did not believe in heaven, but if anyone could attach another world onto this one, it would be his father, who had been a gardener and expert grafter in Vila de São Sebastião, on the island of Terceira in the Azores. Manny had been born in Monterey, where he helped his father bind living trees to each other so that the branches curved to spell out letters—C or S, or K or L—and one time an apple blossomed into a perfect dot to form an "i" until it grew old and fell, though people said of the dotted i, while it lasted, "If you look carefully you'll see the word 'is.'" It had been a good thing to do with his father, who stuttered badly and stopped speaking. Manny never knew quite what to do with the tangle of that silence.

Gemma never had that problem. She and her grandpa had shared a devotion to the movies. It made up for them not being able to tell their own stories back and forth. They went to films so often that Gemma's eyes got uncomfortable outside of dark rooms, and she squinted through daylight. Sometimes, back when Manny was gambling—driving as far as Reno because he'd once been lucky with keno at Harrah's—he would go to the movie theater in town to find them with their heads together, watching the screen. He would stay near the exit. Even then he could not get rid of his betting spirit: If I count to ten, Lord, and she turns around, she'll come home, and if she doesn't, Lord, then fine, she's better off with my father for a while.

Her weeping at her grandpa's funeral had broken Manny in so many places that he sometimes felt gusts of wind were bandages, scarcely holding him together.

He followed the parade through downtown, past the old customs house toward the church, where everyone would file in for Mass. He would stand outside; he hated church. But he liked to see the *vara* go by, the four-sided corral of poles decorated with garlands. Amanda Sousa, the main Festival Queen, was walking inside the vara with her court. At the steps of San Carlos Church, the boys carrying it lifted it high and collapsed the poles together into a lintel for everyone to walk beneath.

"Uncle Manny!" Daisy cried out. She stuck out her tongue and laughed. She was having a delirious time and blew him playacting kisses, pretending to be a queen. In fact, she did have a moneyed but beneficent air—not so different from Queen Isabel of Portugal, who had started the whole idea of Holy Ghost cults long ago. Manny liked very much that far away in California they were still doing as Isabel had asked: she declared that each year, at Pentecost, the poor and hungry had to be fed for free, and the nobility should give them robes and crowns and sit down with them.

"Gemma!" he called, watching his daughter head for the church.

She also blew him a kiss, getting into the act. Being around Daisy was good for her. Today you could make a lucky *promessa*, a barter with the Holy Ghost, and he made one: Please, her name in lights. I will help pay next year to feed everyone, if You do that.

He would wait until next year to rejoin those who said that the expense and competition with the capes was getting away from the idea of being humble and feeding everyone. For now he felt perfectly clear. A person looking at him, out in the hot sunshine, would see that he was slight of build, and it might be surmised that he had a tendency toward ailments of the nerves, but would that person guess that he was forgiving this aspect of human nature, to compete, to dress up, to try to be regal? Would that person know he was finding it noble and touching, that this vow to feed one another for at least one day had remained unbroken since the time of Queen Isabel? How perfectly astonishing, when you thought about it, that people could keep a promise for over six hundred years.

He became bothered when Humberto Vargas, one of his old bookmakers, came up to him in the parish dining hall and said, "What am I, the devil, you say two words to me you're going to hell?"

"Yeah. Something like that."

"Nice cape your girl's got. Been taking your business elsewhere?"

"No," he said, "I haven't."

"Sure," said Humberto, "sure." He clapped a hand on Manny's shoulder and walked away, leaving Manny furious and then anxious.

Maybe playing around with the numbers in Frank's office books counted as gambling. Not a loan. Had he already broken his promise to Gemma? His breathing got shallow. For that matter, what about the business of making a deal with the Holy Ghost? Do this magic trick, and if I get lucky with some net profits I'll pay You back? A dice roll with heaven. Did that count?

Men and women in red aprons were seating people at the long tables and passing bowls with slices of French bread and mint. Everyone took one and waited for the pans of meat, cabbage, and broth to go down the table, and they ladled that over the bread and mint to make a soup. Manny scanned the room, trying to find Gemma. He saw the main queen, Amanda, talking to her father, Joe Sousa. A lot of the food and decorations were donated, but Joe had offered to take his turn this year picking up most of the expenses, and he looked agitated but pleased, like a father at his daughter's wedding. A line stretched out the door, and at the far end of the dining hall, in the open kitchen, men were drinking beer and stirring vats. People were chatting and laughing and arguing and helping each other pass things, and they were sharing wine and Styrofoam cups filled with pickled lupini beans. Someone had gone to the trouble of covering the white paper tablecloths with decals of stars. He wanted to find Gemma, to be with her; the scout was supposed to arrive at any second and everyone knew it; heads were lifting and turning.

Maria Duarte came up behind him and said, "By your lonesome over here, Manny?"

"I'm looking for Gemma. You did a terrific job. Big crowd this year."

"I ever have to put this day together again, I want a whistle and a whip."

They watched covered tureens of the *sopas* being handed out through the kitchen's window, to be loaded onto trucks to go to the housebound or the people who were too sad about their dead to come out. "It's a good thing, all of this," he said.

"It'll be a better thing when Mr. Hollywood shows up," said Maria.

"Not here yet? I was wondering."

"We're all wondering." She did a Mae West wiggle. "Maybe he'll say, Forget these young chickies, honey, it's you we want."

A shout went up for Maria, and she left him by himself again. On one wall the Vieira brothers had put together an elaborate mural made out of netting. They had taken old fishing nets and bunched them up and twisted them into the shapes of humans and boats and fish. They had shaped a lighthouse out of netting and given it an orange light over net-waters. In one net-boat, a net-crowd was hauling in a catch; in a net-rowboat, a net-man and net-woman sat together, not working. They had to be in love. Farther away, a single net-man occupied a third net-boat, not fishing, just off by himself. Each of the three net-boats meant something different: community, romance, and solitude. Manny was glad that the Holy Ghost Festival would happen up and down the valley for a whole season, in other communities, but he was especially glad that the scout had chosen Monterey as the one to visit. Monterey had the ocean backdrop, the view, the clear air, the fishing history, and this mural with the people made of netting.

Gemma tugged at his elbow.

"Got a place saved for me somewhere?" he said. "I'm starving."

"Daddy," she said hotly. "I saw you talking to Humberto."

"For half a minute. Right? It wasn't what you were thinking."

"How do I know that?"

"Because I made you a promise."

"Big deal. You've made lots of promises."

"I am looking you in the eye and telling you the truth," he said.

"I've heard that one before," she said. He lost her in the crowd, couldn't see where she and Daisy and Frank and Glória might be sitting, but now he wasn't hungry anyway; he was feeling short of air. He passed the bar, where the television was playing the Giants game. He stopped and said, "Give me a red wine," and Joe Almeida took his money and poured his drink. The Giants were behind, 3-2, against the Cardinals. He had another glass, this time of green wine, before going outside.

He shouldn't have done that. He was getting disoriented, and he'd risked Gemma catching him near a baseball game right after talking to Humberto. She would never believe he had resisted placing a bet. His hands were trembling. Because he'd had an urge to do exactly that, make some fast money to put back in Frank's petty-cash fund so that he could be past any chance of unpleasantness.

He could get some shrimp or crab at the *tasca* set up near the auction stage. Booths were selling ceramic plates and T-shirts that said, "Kiss Me, I'm Portuguese" and "Monterey IDES, 2000 AD." Another booth offered *fado* and *chamaritta* cassette tapes, and another had the *quermesse*: old ladies tightly rolled hundreds of square-inch scraps of white paper that they then bent in the middle. Manny was tempted to pay a dollar for five out of a fishbowl and unroll them to see if he had one with a number that would match a prize. Most of the stuff was junk—white-elephant donations—but there was also a money tree. This was innocent festival play, but he never knew what would send him into that old desire. Rose Bettencourt, behind the counter, said, "Manny, cheapskate, buy some chances."

"No thanks, Rose," he said. To make conversation—she was always moaning about her health—he added, "Good job rolling all those papers, what with your arthritis."

She held out her hand and said, "Arthritis? Get over here."

"Jesus, Rose. Relax. What, you want to arm wrestle?"

"Come here and test my grip."

"No."

"I don't see this hand dropping." She stood there as if she'd said hello and he was being rude. He went to shake her hand and be done with her, but her grip was brutal. She had a shock of iron hair and a bosom built of stone. He would be a bad guy if he overpowered her but a weakling if he didn't. What was it with people? Always ready to squeeze you until your bones broke.

"Hey, you win," he said.

"Ha," she said, letting him go. "OK, I give you now some free chances. You're a good sport."

"Nothing there I want to win, Rose."

"We got here a money tree and potholders and waffle irons not outta the box. My booth don't need your insults."

She thrust the chances into his hand, and he was clutching them when Frank showed up and said, "That's a nice money tree."

He held up the chances in his hand and said, "This is a charity booth at a festival, Frank, and these are a gift. Aren't they, Rose?"

"My lips are sealed. I say I'm giving away free chances, I get my ass run outta the business."

"Listen, Manny," said Frank. And then Manny disappeared into some chamber where he was submerged and the sound of Frank's voice was barely getting through. Something about Frank planning to bid on a painting to be auctioned by Aquatic Galleries. An underwater artwork. Frank was going to bid on it for the office, an empty space over a reception table. "You'll need to write me a check from petty cash tomorrow," said Frank, "because we'll be having an outside auditor come in and look through everything so we can get that loan."

"What loan?" said Manny.

"You getting senile? We talked about it last week, remember, for the new wing I'm adding to the store? Lamps, plates, linens. Everything you could want indoors, I'm thinking. Not just furniture."

Manny knew he was panicking, drunk on an empty stomach; his chest began to heave. He had lost his ability to put on a good poker face. He told himself to calm down. Frank was his boss; he often bought things for the office from petty cash. He was not trying to trap or test him. But why was Frank bringing this up now, with Manny standing there with a fistful of bazaar chances?

"Manny? You hearing me?"

"Why wouldn't I be?"

Across the lawn men on the auction stage were setting up crates of produce, flats of peppers and figs for the first round of bidding. People were gathering on the benches. Manny saw Gemma without her cape on, and he said, "Excuse me, Frank," and went to her, the little paper chances falling from his wet fist onto the grass. He said, "Gemma? Honey? Why aren't you wearing your cape?"

"Because it's four million degrees out, Daddy. Daisy isn't wearing hers either."

"You know," he said, lowering his voice, "that scout might already be here. Wouldn't it be nice if he sees you in it and—well, anything could happen for you."

"I wish you'd stop that."

He never knew what to say to her. Her grandpa couldn't speak to her either, but their speechlessness was profoundly full of stories and images, as if inspiration and aspiration, the twin glories of movies, were caught in the breath and lit up on-screen. Manny had a craving to win this day that made him groggy, as if desire and heat like this were too much for his frame.

"Daddy?" said Gemma. "You look terrible."

"No," he said. "No, I'm fine, darling."

But she went to find her cape hanging from a tree branch, and for a moment, his eyesight swimming, it looked as if Gemma might as well have cracked open one of the letters made of fruited branches on those grafted trees and some long-trapped, long-captured, long-repressed dream of spelling itself out in full was pouring out in a rush of blood-red and cloud-white. She put on the cape, and people backed away, looking at her.

Frank sat with Glória and Daisy on another bench as Carlos Dutra, the auctioneer, began prattling. Manny reminded himself that today was the day for everyone to be fed, and he hadn't eaten. He could still go to the dining hall, but he did not want to miss the scout. The sound of numbers, amounts, people bidding higher and higher, Frank's voice chiming in, increased the sense that his head was liquid and sloshing back and forth, and he had a thought so ignoble, so horrifying, that he clutched his hands because they were going to fly up as if to get as far as possible from his mind: he could ask Gemma for a loan. They could raid her money-market fund, her college money, and put five thousand dollars back into the petty-cash fund, and he could find a way of explaining to the outside auditor the consistency of the error; he would invent a hundred-dollar-a-week need for more office supplies. That would work.

Gemma sat next to him again, wearing her cape, and her hand reached up to wipe the side of his face. "Daddy?" she said.

He glanced toward the auctioneer, offering an enormous seascape, and Frank's voice was in counterpoint to the voice of a woman who also wanted it: one hundred, three hundred, five hundred; the audience was gasping and applauding. Manny got up and said to Gemma, "I'd better get something to eat, precious," and on his way to the tasca with seafood, a small woman in a polka-dot blouse and white linen slacks, probably a cousin of the Sousa family, said to him, "Show me the nearest food, I'm dying," and he said, "Come with me." The woman was scary-skinny, like all the Sousas, and he said, "Let me," and he bought her a plate of crab fritters and shrimp and scallops with garlic. "This is the good stuff, so we pay for this, to raise money for the poor," he said, thinking that he should eat also, but he couldn't. Strange; his appetite was there, but the effort of feeding himself seemed too much. He heard Frank's voice, offering eight hundred dollars for the painting, and he saw himself writing the check for it. He was already on to tomorrow and wanted today to be finished, the results in.

"This is nice of you," said the woman, and slid her dark glasses onto the top of her head. She ate with a plastic fork, and when she finished, she said, "Thanks for feeding me in such grand style. These are the best scallops I've ever had."

"Right out of the ocean," he said. "That's the beauty of Monterey."

She thanked him again and said that she wanted to watch the auction for a while.

He stayed inside the little shed and watched the cooks frying clams in hot oil, and when he walked outside again, the bidding was over and Frank was smiling. Eight hundred dollars for a seascape. What was it like, to have that kind of money? He wondered again if Frank already knew the truth and was trying to frighten him into an admission; that would be just like Frank, to require a beseeching for forgiveness. Then Manny was startled: a large bald man with a briefcase was talking to Gemma.

All the planning, the week-by-week writing of those checks—and now that the moment was here, just like that, time collapsed. The man walked around Gemma, who held her cape out for him to take in. He stepped back to view it, and Manny thought, Thank you, thanks, next year I'll pay for everything, I'll feed everyone.

But that brought the panic back, too, because Frank might fire him tomorrow or press charges, and Glória would certainly side with Frank. Money, to Glória, was much thicker than blood. But Gemma was going to be in pictures, and he could live with finding another job. That would be for the best anyway. He would be inspired to do better for himself, now that Gemma was taken care of. He might still have a brainstorm between now and facing the outside auditor, some way of explaining the ongoing one-hundred-dollar debit. Frank's company was doing well. No one needed to be punished with jail, but now that didn't matter. Manny could do time, if he had to.

It took all of his strength to let Gemma alone to do the talking. He had a sense that barreling over there now, chatting with the bald man with the briefcase, would tip fate the wrong way. Gemma was grinning, nodding at the man.

Manny tried to read her face but couldn't after the bald man shook Gemma's hand and walked away. She sat down again to follow the auction: someone had donated wooden toy trucks. A man shouted, Ten dollars, then came twenty, twenty-five, thirty dollars. Manny spotted the man with the briefcase on a fold-out chair, and he forced himself to walk slowly until he was next to him, and he said, "I saw you admiring my daughter."

"That's quite a cape," he said. "Something else."

"Yes," said Manny. He had a speech ready, a shameless one; he was ready to beg the man to select Gemma. He was waiting for the man to say who he was, to explain that Gemma would be on a plane to Los Angeles next week, and Manny could forgo pleading and say in a dignified manner that he understood the role would be small but that didn't matter, when the man said, "Looks like the scout has found her girl."

"What?" said Manny.

The man pointed toward the small blond woman with the polka-dot blouse who was standing next to Daisy, Frank, and Glória. Manny's sister was doing little leaps in the air while squealing. When Gemma arrived on the scene with them, the blond woman knelt to lift up and examine the cape Manny had bought. Gemma looked happy. Daisy's face was radiant, as always, but now her radiance wore an extra gloss, a thing made more itself by being found.

"I thought you were the scout," said Manny.

"No, said the bald man. "No. Why would you think that?"

What, thought Manny, I fed that tiny woman scallops, now she has to put my daughter in the movies? How could a savior be so thin and small? More than that, he had not considered the possibility that Frank, who already had so much, should win this time, too.

Gemma ran to him and said, "Daddy! The lady wants to rent my cape. She says it's the most beautiful cape in the world! She wants Daisy to wear it in the movie."

"You should wear your cape. It's yours."

"It'll still be mine," said Gemma, "but I'm glad it'll be Daisy wearing it. She loves the attention. You can tell. I get stage fright."

"You'll get over it."

"My cape is going to be there for everyone to see," said Gemma, reaching for her father's trembling hand. He was staring at Frank and Glória and Daisy celebrating, and Gemma said, "Thanks, Daddy."

He looked at her and bowed his head. What had he ever done, to be rewarded with such a generous girl? He did not know what to say, because numbers were crowding out any words. He had a few hours before the auditor would be staring at Manny's work. Frank could be in a fine mood, his daughter tapped by the great outer powers, and Frank would still send his brother-in-law to jail. At some point, Manny would have to tell Gemma the truth, and he would have to agree with her: Daisy was open, happy, inflamed, eager, not the most stunning girl but the most alive presence—far and away the most spirited, the one most likely to find an inspired moment with a camera eye on her. He had known Daisy her whole life and not quite seen that, but this scout had figured it out in minutes. He despised the clarity and fairness of it; of course Daisy was meant to win all along.

Still—he and Gemma could go to the movies together, when his debt was somehow paid. If he had to go to jail, it would not be forever. If the film were ever finished, they could sit together in the dark theater and listen to everyone sharply inhale to see such splendor. They would know, the two of them, where it had first come from. There would probably be a point in the movie when his niece would turn away from the camera and only the cape would be on view; the star right then could be anyone. What would be the harm, if he said to his daughter in those rapid few seconds: There you are. That's really you, darling.

That night he lay awake, wondering how he would face the terrors of the next morning, everything he had done laid bare. He was rehearsing how to ask Glória, and Frank, and Gemma, for forgiveness, when he heard Gemma shrieking.

He ran to her room and switched on the light. She was having a nightmare, she said; someone was holding her down where she could barely breathe, and she'd been trying to get to the surface and wake up but couldn't. She was sitting up in bed now, shaking.

"I can tell you what that is," he said. "Your grandpa explained it to me when I was a boy. It's called *o Pesadelo com a Mão Furada*. That means the Nightmare with the Drilled Hand."

"Yes, it was like a hand over my face," she said. She was sweating.

He sat on the edge of her bed. "Is it like having Grandpa here with you, to learn this?" he asked.

She nodded.

"It feels as if the hand holding you down has only a drill mark in the palm, and you inhale all panicky through it while you're trying to swim up to where you can be awake."

"Yes," she said, "that's it."

"It makes you feel horribly alone. But my father used to tell me, it will give you compassion when you find out everyone in the world goes through it."

"Does it happen just once?" she asked.

He told her that the Nightmare with the Drilled Hand was a trial of childhood, so she would think it would go away soon and never return. That was a lie. He had had many Nightmares with the Drilled Hand since he had fallen in love three years before with a married woman. Their affair had lasted only nine months. But sometimes, even now, he was so struck by the image of this woman locked naked in his embrace that it staggered him. He might be in a line at the bank and would have to grip the velvet rope. He might be in a grocery store and would need to brace himself against a ledge of produce. Mostly it happened while he was figuring the net totals for his rich brother-in-law, when he felt porous and as stringlike as the lines on the pages of his accounting books. What was he then, eight hours a day, except some fishing snare meant to catch errors? How do we all manage it, he often wondered, walking around as self-possessed as we do?

"Daddy," said Gemma, and put her arms around him, "I thought I was going to die."

He held his daughter close.

The truth, he knew, is that love never comes again in the same way, and often it never comes again at all. And even when the gift of it is there, in your arms, something in love cannot resist leaning toward your ear to whisper. It whispers that it's a temporary blessing, it always is, and soon it will be—not gone, not that, that would be more of a relief—it will be dissolving into the very air around you, the air that becomes a labor to breathe.

The Knife Longs for the Ruby

This work of fiction is inspired by the true story of a nineteenth-century statue known as one of the most touching images of Christ in the world. The sculpture lies on white silk in Brazil, in the city of Salvador's Igreja da Nossa Senhora do Carmo.

Tónio, his hair combed stiffly upward into a turban shape and glued in place with honey, set the decanter of *cachaça* on a tarnished silver tray. He carried it into the study, where the priest lay in his hammock. Father Jaime got drunk exactly one night a week, and he did it very beautifully, falling into the sparkling glass of firewater and emerging out the other end, clarified and wounded.

Tónio had once asked why he did it, and Father Jaime replied, "So that I don't drink every waking minute." Tónio nodded; he himself visited the prostitutes in the city in order to bear the solitude of the country.

The heat dripped a film of honey over Tónio's eyes, painting a golden blanket over the furniture. His pores soaked up the sweetness, but nothing cured his hunger.

Father, what should I do to stop being hollow as a drum?
I'm hollow, too, Toninho; I just make louder the music of my skin.

Tónio frowned as he removed an untouched plate of red snapper from Father Jaime's desk. The priest was fifty and aging rapidly, one of those frail Lisbon blonds with a high forehead that made it look as if his thoughts were scuffling. Tónio handed the first glassful to Father Jaime and retreated to the hard flat bed in his stone *senzala*, detached from the main house, until queasiness drove him back to the hammock, to reach through the chrysalis of netting to wipe away the alcohol poking through Father Jaime's skin in shining beads. He was posed in flight, arms wide. Tónio rubbed coconut oil into the priest's parched hands. Father Jaime never stirred, but Tónio imagined that this was the touch that told the priest it was time to come back. Tónio took the statue of Iemenjá out of the drawer; letting the black-faced goddess preside was his own little rebellion. He wasn't brave like the slaves fleeing the sugarcane plantations and setting up colonies in the jungle; he had no idea how to survive in the wild. He was thirty, an ancient house pet.

The air alone made Tónio ready to burst: *Ai*, look at dawn over the *jaca* trees! Shades of coral, like a fleet of crabs cracked and de-shelled.

Father Jaime, waking up, touched his head to see if it was still attached. He sighed; it was. He opened the curtains, a gray brocade of dirt and bugs. He kissed Iemenjá before shutting her back in the drawer. She made him grin. He sat down to write his stories, but even bathed in cachaça from a brain on fire, his characters remained wooden.

Pineapples like eyeless heads: green hair, scaly skin. The clay earth red with welts from their push to emerge. Toninho wielding a machete, carving the sky into fanciful animals. Father Jaime thinning the plants, adding soil that had passed through the intestines of earthworms. Ever since his expulsion from the Jesuits, he and

Toninho had earned their modest keep by growing pineapples in a spot without a name, called the-place-outside-Salvador.

Tónio visited the distant hills of the city only in darkness. He'd been there last night. But what did women look like during the day? Why had he never tried to find out? He swung his machete fiercely. Imagine that: women walking on the black-and-white cobblestones! Going to the market! Buying copper flowers!

He screamed as the machete sliced into his leg.

Father Jaime ran to him. He didn't have to ask what had happened. On the mornings after Tónio had combed the Ladeira da Conceição for whores, he was frequently in the throes of sleep, of peril. The cut wasn't deep, but Father Jaime carried him into the house to bathe and dress the wound. Had he made love without rest, or had he hurt himself because of that ridiculous honey pouring into his eyes? What a silly fashion for house slaves to do their hair up like the capoeira fighters, just so their owners could feel guarded by someone tough.

He washed Tónio's hair with almond soap and rinsed it with well water. He hadn't done this since Toninho was a newborn, when he'd rescued him from a rich family whose maid, an unwed mother, had died giving birth.

Tónio kept scratching his head; it was too bare. He sobbed that he felt too light and birds would carry him off.

"Stop your nonsense," said Father Jaime. "It's time you found some self-respect so that one of us will have it."

Tónio suspected that this referred to his forays to the whores, and in case he missed the point—this he found a bit insulting—Father Jaime pointed to an enormous oblong of rosewood that some noble had given him in exchange for some prayers and said, "Make yourself busy scraping a statue out of that." All Europeans, not just the religious ones, were like children in thinking that manual labor got rid of sexual desire.

The wood was thoroughly reddish, saturated with the blood of the tree. Father Jaime had considered carving a trunk out of it, but he lacked any talent as a sculptor. The block was like his faith: featureless, a weight. Tónio knelt on the knee of his unwounded leg. Water dripped onto his shoulders. He smoothed the surface with his hand; the rosewood appeared to be suffering.

The wood was firm, but deep down it was tender and only blunt knives would serve. He had no idea what form to give the rosewood; it had not told him what was locked inside itself yet, only that it was paralyzed with the fear of pain. He spoke to it and realized with a start that if words were coming out of him he must not be completely empty.

But talking to the wood every afternoon caused stabbing pains in his stomach. That made sense. The priest wrote stories with letters drawn like miniature swords, so speaking must be a type of battle. Tónio cornered Father Jaime and burst out with, "I need to go to the marketplace in daylight to buy ginger to chew. If you want extra work out of me, I'll need my strength, please, Father."

The priest gave him money and sent him toward the hills and the sea.

Look at the shrimp boats that rise and fall under the burden of their wet catch . . .

He wobbled around like a drunk. The light at the marketplace of Salvador stabbed needles through the black dots of his eyes to stitch burning threads into his skull, and the stalls dazzled with everything he could imagine—tobacco, Brazil nuts, birds-of-paradise cut so you could hear the stems shrieking, feathers, beads—until blinding tears stopped him dead. A woman wrapped in a purple cloth printed with orchids broke through the nimbus, gripped his arm, and said, "Why are you crying?"

He suddenly was beyond words. His head dropped onto the forehead she offered, and they froze into the prettiest statue he could dream up. Was love abrupt and specific, did it take a single guise, a particular shape; did it require both the giving up and the giving of everything? Her flesh had the heat of actual sun, not the coolness of the moon. Her name was Teresa Silva. She was a slave set free because she'd stuffed a thousand cuttlefish with a mix of shrimps' eyes, and the guests of her master had collapsed into a type of ecstasy. It was fashionable now for nobles to release their slaves for artistic feats. Freedom meant living in a thatched hut with her parents and frying bean cakes for money, cutting life close to the bone.

May I make love to you, Teresa?

Yes. I could use that.

While he kissed her, she whispered a warning. She'd been in love with a writer who lived on the bluffs overlooking the bay, someone with a few drops of slave blood himself. He'd gone back to his wife and his fame, and Teresa, who hadn't seen him in a year, desperately wanted the passion for him to leave her muscles. Tónio adored even this test. He'd never known perfect love, but he was convinced it required the embracing of flaws. He forgot to buy the ginger.

Among the palm trees, the sand thrumming with fleas leaping up to watch, he sank his mouth onto her and held on before spilling what felt like the entire contents of himself over her belly.

Perhaps the problem was that he was much too full.

He stroked the rosewood with two blunt knives. He would speed Teresa's recovery from the writer by creating an artwork of his own. The wood gave out tiny cries like a child coming out of sleep.

As a boy in Lisbon Father Jaime had emptied his own *pinico* rather than leave it for the servants. Pouring his filth into the gutter had penetrated him with a shame that followed him here and made him one with the nobles in the city who pretended they had no stomachs, and one with the slaves forced to carry whale-oil lanterns under the cover of night to empty their masters' pinicos, risking dysentery and skin rot.

The nobles took pride in never leaving their houses: who could bear the sun-baked stench of bodily horror?

When Father Jaime came to hear their confessions, they sometimes ventured onto porches.

A man with a white goatee, a rheum-brimmed eye, dealing whiskey-stained cards. *Father, forgive me; unto you I place my crime of gambling.*

A roustabout eating candied lemon slices, pinching the slave girl fanning him: *Father, forgive me; unto you I place my crime of lust.*

The Reis family sent their palanquin to bring him to their Scandinavian-style house. Their crystal lamps were shaped like ice formations. Father Jaime's sin was his ingratitude, because this family's manner of atonement was to exchange his pathetic crop of pineapples for supplies, cloth and food and cachaça and gardening tools, sending provisions on the backs of these same slaves now bearing the priest on the palanquin, never mentioning the cost when the pineapples didn't cover what was needed, all so that neither Father Jaime nor Tónio had to face their ineptitude at bargaining and their timidity at large.

He entered the bedroom, where the curtains, rucked from sweaty grasping, looked like the pictures of intestines in his book about anatomy. He hid it in his closet but often caught Tónio paging through it. His excuse for keeping it was that since the first publishing venture in Brazil had been to print playing cards for the nobles, even a scandalous book was a step forward.

Senhora Reis, propped up in bed, sweated in her Parisian fur. She was made of paste, you could crush her with a single blow. "Bless me, Father, for I have sinned," she wheezed when he bowed his ear near her rum-vapored mouth. She ticked off minor offenses: lies, petty coveting.

He gave the Te Absolvo but wanted to roar back the largeness of her errors. Where had his courage drained out? He'd raised such a fuss in the rectory back in Rio that the other Jesuits had ushered, rushed, thrown him out: their system of using slaves to harvest sugarcane was successful, they were competing with the plantations, they didn't need a blond boy from Europe pointing out at every turn how the laws of Brazil were heading toward emancipation.

"Go free yourself," the Bishop had said. "Go preach to pineapples."

Senhora Reis told Father to look under her bed. He blushed. He knelt and winced at the clutter gilded with dust and said, "Yes?"

"The ice skates," she said. "Give them to your little houseboy."

"He's my son," said Father Jaime. He held up the leather strap with its dangling steel prize. The blades were dull and the boots stained after their long glide from Norway. He smiled at Senhora Reis weakly. He'd been full of brave talk when he was young, but he wasn't a leader, he was merely someone who had once resisted, a husk of a priest shielding a husk of a man.

Senhor Reis offered him pineapple laid out in spokes on a Chinese plate. He had given Father Jaime a sack of rubies a year ago in thanks for absolution after confessing a love affair. The priest kept the rubies at the bottom of a closet at home; what to do with them?

He ate the pineapple because he loved it even though it gave him hives and cold sores; he adored its oozing of bright yellow wine.

That night Tónio lanced the boils on Father Jaime's face, arms, and chest. "You've been eating pineapple," he said. "Naughty child."

Or was the redness from the scourge of collected sins? Wasn't mortification, the need to humiliate the body, supposed to recapture the missing half of his soul? "Is it terribly disgusting?" Father Jaime asked.

"Yes, but I don't mind," said Tónio. They knew each other too well not to say the truth. The sores spewed clear and scarlet jewels of illness, and Tónio washed his hands afterward, lest he, too, suffer a similar itch of skin and infect Teresa. Strange joy flooded him: he'd lived so long with the priest that here was proof that they were as matched as clockwork. Their insides were exploding at the same time.

A woman dashed from the crowd with a shard of glass and slashed Father Jaime's bare chest. He yelped under a whip, and the bystanders applauded. Blood rolled down like melting roses onto his trousers and sandals, and his face heated up inside the sack over his head, held in place with a rope around his neck. Tónio had embroidered bees around the eyeholes in yellow thread.

Father Jaime didn't believe that his cuts released the collected sins of his penitents along with his own offenses, and he wondered if the other priests and city officials in the parade held to that conceit. Tónio probably thought he marched to atone for drinking, but that, too, was wrong. He consented to this nonsensical torment once a year so that the flashes of glass could remind him that he still owned a body. No one in Brazil, not even Tónio, knew that in his twenties back in Lisbon he'd been enthralled with his wife, and when she died in childbirth with their only child, a girl who also perished, he decided to leave the mortal realm, and only in the priesthood can a man hide and yearn for the invisible; love would never again have a form for him. He drank not out of sorrow anymore—his darling had dissolved over time, the baby had never solidified into an entity— but because silence itself was increasingly shapeless, and drinking made it jagged.

The guitarists bashed out, "Maiden, Maiden, My Beloved."

Street boys pelted Father Jaime with cashews.

The distant ocean was like a ransom of dissolved emeralds.

Sore, swathed in bandages, he attended a concert of African choirboys led by a Frenchman from Marseille, singing the *Stabat Mater*. The charm of their conjoined voices would gainsay their freedom.

His truest sin was in holding on to Toninho, pretending that they were a family. Five years ago the congress had passed the Law of the Free Womb to liberate the babies born to slaves, and now that it was 1874, it was time to realize in the flesh the quarrel he'd started long ago with the Jesuits.

He found him at home, coaxing what looked like a pair of legs out of the end of the rosewood: like a woman opening them in delivery? Could Tónio read him that well?

"Are you in love, Toninho?" he asked.

The slave turned in fright and said, "How did you know, Father?" He was tall and thin as a sapling, with the unprotected, moist face of a salamander.

"I can tell," said the priest. "It might be my one talent. Go marry her and have some children."

"Not until I finish this."

"Te absolvo. Finish it for a house of your own."

"No, Father," said Tónio. He squeezed the handles of the blunt knives and looked away. He did not care to admit that he needed to take his time, to ensure that Teresa would be finished with her old love and ready for his. He would die without this distraction. "The statue will be for you, to stay in the field where you say Mass, since my leaving will mean you are alone."

Father Jaime tried to continue writing his stories, episodes set in a medieval Lisbon suffused with the languid disease of afternoons. He burned all his pages and wrote for the first time about his wife (though not very well), and also out of nowhere he scrawled, *Where will Toninho survive? The province of Bahía swarms with cattle rustlers, cutthroats, mystics, troubadours.*

I have figured out why he is using two useless knives: he understands that taking more pains to create something can add to the sheer pleasure of offering it up to the universe.

Perhaps there comes a moment when one's own wants give way toward the inspiration of God's will, when one begins to let go, and in the letting go something happens. Creation was speaking through him and calling him to it. And it struck Father Jaime that God the Father had been the one waiting, waiting for him to take hold and help complete His creation. There was a child inside God Himself, and it looked like Father Jaime, it looked like everyone.

W hile diving Tónio saw the legs and swollen head of an oc-
topus palpitating in a crevice. He stopped to console it.
It was the reduction of himself in love: crammed inside Teresa . . .
three months with her. A season. She kissed his machete wound, its
purple marbling his leg. Love must be physical. Harm insists upon
the physical. The statue sprouted veins and uplifted knees . . . while
carving the rosewood he marveled that Teresa's absence actually
burnished his love; how frightening that love yearns for a vastness
to swallow its contradictions.

On the feast day of Iemenjá he bought Teresa a comb, a red lipstick, and a paper boat decorated with sleepy Phoenician eyes. She
giggled and waved good-bye while launching the boat filled with the
trinkets. The shoreline's contour shifted, buzzed with everyone else
sending gifts to the goddess, who was terribly sweet but vain and
liked her adornments. The sea was a docile animal, taking hundreds
of paper boats on its back without flicking its tail.

He grabbed her hand and watched their offering sail off and sink
into the arms of Iemenjá, and said, "When I finish a sculpture, you'll
come to live with me."

"With you and a priest?" She crossed herself and laughed.

They walked backward from the water because it was dangerous
to stop facing Iemenjá, and as he sorted his thoughts to devise the
lines that would convey that he was taking his time with the carving
so that her obsession over her former lover would be done, by which
time he would earn his freedom for her, and . . . she turned her back
on Iemenjá to study the bluff, and he spun her around, but too late,
she was a pillar of salt, and he was a pillar of stone: wasn't the bluff
where that writer lived? High up, drinks in hand, striped umbrellas
at a tilt like huge blooms; the writer and his polished friends were
spying upon the celebration of the goddess; they were no bigger
than sand bugs from where Tónio stood stockstill. Teresa took such
care not to stare toward the party in the sky that all he could sense
was the party in the sky.

"Oh, good! Look!" she cried, and ran to join some friends on a square of cloth on the beach. They had the brightly anxious look of the recently free, and one ex-slave had hard-boiled yellow eyes from drinking. They passed a whiskey bottle, and Teresa took a sip and thrust it at Tónio, and he said, "No, thanks."

"Oh, he's sulking. I do believe he asked me to marry him."

"Marry him? Do you like pineapple juice, Terezinha?" said one boy, who seemed like a capoeira fighter.

Merriment in gales.

"He could never marry me," said Teresa. "He's grown up taking care of a saint. And I'm no saint!"

"Are you a saint?" the capoeira boy asked Tónio.

"No, no," said Teresa. Was she already drunk? "He *lives* with a saint. He's a saint for taking care of a—saint!" she shrieked.

He flinched when she punched his arm. "He's not what you think," said Tónio, and he hollowed out as the words left him, sketching the picture for Teresa and these strangers about the priest getting inebriated every Friday night, flying into oblivion. Tónio took a swig of whiskey to demonstrate how the priest drank, and the burning cut through Tónio and, in a panic to get away, to get out of his own skin, he jumped up and stumbled backward, this wasn't the priest falling but himself, and they roared and pointed at him because humiliation, after all, must be physical before it can start to leech the spirit.

He righted himself and said, "Come to me."

Baby, baby, the capoeira fighter sang.

Teresa laughed and said, "Look but don't touch."

Tónio lunged and held onto her arm while she twisted and screamed, *Let me go, let me go,* and when he did he saw the bruises his fingers had left on her skin.

Let me kiss you. I'm sorry. Let me kiss your arm.

You've done enough to me. Kiss the air.

He dropped down cross-legged. He was petrified past moving as Teresa left with her friends. She slapped the top of his head in a way that was half affectionate, and that's what made him cry. He didn't bother to wipe his face. The towels of everyone on the beach got folded up. The boats all sank to Iemenjá while he dreamt up a better ending, one beautiful enough to enable him to unhinge his arms and legs so that he could start back toward home. He decided that his invented good-bye should contain a few contours of truth: he was kissing the back of her neck while tears ran in sheets down her face as she gazed toward the bluff at the women in their French dresses, their skirts lifting in the air that might have been hers. She whispered, *Farewell. But now you know me beyond fathoming, since you're feeling what I've carried with me all along.*

Oh, love, you might have been mine got chiseled onto his skeleton.

When Tónio next prepared the cachaça, Father Jaime was not in his hammock but at his desk. He looked up at Tónio trembling and said, "I won't be needing that, Toninho, thanks. I think I don't need it ever again, don't you agree?" He glanced back down at his writing.

"Father," said Tónio, startled, rigid. No freedom was possible from someone who could peer into his soul. "I've decided to make the statue into a Christ taken off his crucifix. A priest should have that."

Father Jaime took off his wire-rimmed glasses and smiled. "You might just be the kindest person alive," he said.

Tónio stared into the glittering glass. The fumes rose like invisible reeds. "Even now, Father, you give me the delight of knowing that you're completely wrong."

Father Jaime wrote into the night, revising a story about his wife. He added in their quarrels, boredom, and vacant time until he was wretched with missing her. He would not drink anymore, now that she was in the room, not only for fear of her reproach, but because he would die before sullying the writing of her name with an unsteady hand.

T he hours spilled from their numerical confines. In the second year of closing himself in to work on the statue, Tónio indulged a passion for the harsh tobacco of Bahía. The statue softened, forgave him for trying to use it to woo someone. He passed through being in love into being in love with love, and finally he pushed past the dangers of being enamored with abstractions and felt the lacerations of normal life: he and Father Jaime whitewashed the main house and repainted the yellow trim around the windows, swept the senzala, and did not discuss why Tónio never went out anymore.

They laundered the curtains, dusted the books.

Ate lightly, tapioca with papaya.

Tónio ran into Teresa once, in the Mercado Modelo, and bought her a calico dress.

She was going to marry someone—not her writer—who could buy her lots of clothing—none of it grand. He stroked her shoulder as he might have done if they'd grown old together. The great amorphous horror was not that people disappeared or died, but that they found so little to perish for.

I'll picture you wearing that dress, Senhora. He bowed.

You touched the dress that will touch me. Good-bye again.

She ran off. Was she giggling? Crying? How could he not be sure? Blood surged into his temples. How stiff in body and sloppy of heart to have bowed.

In the fourth year of carving the statue, so that Tónio could continue without letup, Father Jaime ventured by himself to the marketplace to buy resin that would gloss the wood into skin. The sun toughened his face while he learned how to bargain, cracked him open, and, hatched, alone, he swung the machete in the fields until his back, arms, and legs hurt their way into strength.

In the sixth year Father Jaime published his stories about marriage in a small book with an embossed leather cover. At a party in a house on a bluff, he met a well-known author, Maurício Lima da Jardim, who'd written about his great-great-grandfather's escape from slavery. He was beige and lanky, and Father Jaime Pereira, perching shyly on a cane chair during the party, drinking mango juice, watched the women, black, white, mulatto, fawn over the famous host. The priest did not speak to him, but he admired how Maurício possessed whatever came in front of him; he did not have to search for it, as Father Jaime did; all he had to do was focus on what arrived. Maurício's wife had a compelling texture. She and the priest exchanged nods. The scars of her marriage had sliced into her in a way that no one else should fathom.

Tónio had been postponing working on the statue's face. He caressed the eyes, the vulnerable mouth, until the wood turned into his flesh and then into flesh of its own, and he massaged the sinewy arms with the resin until the pores opened, but it was not until the eighth year of carving with the two blunt knives that, without his touch, the pores opened on their own.

When the Christ was done, it brought Tónio no comfort; it pierced him with a sense of being forsaken, for if mystery seeks creation, definition, then how can it approach the limitless God? What a cruel joke. What was the point of letting go of your own will, letting God have His way, letting inspiration sweep in, if there was no physical love as solace? *God,* he howled. *Why won't you surprise me?*

In 1883, when electric lights were inaugurated in the city of Campos in the province of Rio, the first such lights in Brazil, Father Jaime Pereira helped the servant he called his son, António Pereira, lift the statue onto pillows. Even in death it appeared to be in awful too-serene pain.

Father Jaime had not known his faith had been nonexistent until now that he had it for the first time. He took the sack of rubies from his closet and gave it to Tónio and said, "Go live well. Buy a house overlooking the sea. You'll find someone. Ha, my dear young man. Now with some gems to your name, you'll have women all over you."

"I could touch the bottom of the sea," said Tónio. "I could rise past the houses on the bluff, my Father." His legs were ready to give out from under him. He was spent. "All of that would be smaller than your love for me and my love for you."

While contemplating his freedom Tónio rolled cigarettes and smoked on his bed in his senzala. The spirals of smoke were a superior sculpture, formless and dissipating, and haloed his unbound hair and his leg with that old cut from the machete that throbbed in the night breeze. What prayers could he recite? None of them was enough to match the blasphemous cry of Christ on the cross against God: Why should people be made so?

He ran to the shed to search for the hammer. He looked on the shelves; it wasn't hanging in its usual place.

The hammer was cowering among the pineapples. He laughed out loud: Ho, trying to escape, are you? He took it back to the senzala where he had spent his thirty-eight years and smashed the sack over and over to pulverize the rubies. He glued the blood-red dust over the loincloth and thighs of the reclining Christ. And now it was finished. *Thank you for surprising Me,* God said to him, *for I am terribly alone and tired.* Tónio's one regret was that the dull knives that had done all the work for eight years never had, and never would, be granted anything to do with the rubies. He would not say good-bye to Father Jaime, because there could be no parting between them. He lay down beside the ache of Christ, his head on the hungry ribcage, tucked near the pulse of the carved neck, and he fell deeply in love with this living thing given to him, this beautiful sorrowing creation, and death came for him hardly a heartbeat after he closed his eyes.

To love fiercely, to shepherd a soul, to heal
Is to become the Father yourself

The Mandarin Question

I was born the day my father shot and killed my mother. I was two months premature, but in the hospital my mother's sister would plunge her fingers into the gloves built to hang like bright blue udders inside of the glass box where I was nothing but pale orange blood and damp tissue wrapped with strings. The idea was to hold someone like me, constantly, to fall asleep with your forehead on the glass but to stay there, stay and hold me, so I'd hitch on to the point of growing. I believe that saved my life, having hands on my skin from the start, even ones covered with rubber. They come gloveless for me even now, in daylight and at nighttime.

My Tia Clara was a widow who raised me in her house, where we had a huge print of Saint Rita with a ray connecting her forehead to the forehead of the crucified Lord. We owned a glorious plastic tablecloth with grinning artichokes, some with horn-rimmed spectacles and some with bonnets, under a banner declaring, *Welcome*

to Castroville, Artichoke Capital of the World! I could never refrain from stabbing my fork tines where the plastic thorns poked out of the tips of the leaves. Every Christmas, even when I was tiny, Tia Clara poured me a shot glass of Amaretto because to me it was the color of summer sunsets boiled down and to her it was the crimson of the ribbons she tied tight around packages, and we laughed for the rest of the day, spinning like red tops. We kept pink silk roses. Light dust became their pollen. The nuns in school said, *Remember, man, that you are dust!* and Lisa Gonsalves and I thought that was a scream because it meant in the fields we walked on a million men and the powder of men salted our eyes and we breathed deeply to coat our wet lungs with them and hoped the mud this made would harden to stay inside us, and when we ran our hands through our hair men fed on our scalps. Or lifted away on a breeze.

What wrecked Tia Clara was when her baby brother, Vincent, got called out of the reserves and stepped on a landmine in Afghanistan. *Don't go, don't move, stay here, Faye, don't leave me, you're all I have left,* she sobbed. I was sixteen. I owed her. To move as little as possible, I took up the violin so at least I could agitate the air around me. How did someone dream up a smooth shape with a hole in its center that requires a touch most people cannot manage without producing a screech? But when you learn the touch, the sound turns into a living creature that weeps right there on your shoulder. That's why violinists always shut their eyes at some point when their bow sings, because there's no mortal sight worth having when you're stroking a creature that's crying.

I played my violin at the job I got after school at the entrance to the slaughterhouse. There's this thing called dark-cutting. It's plain biology. When an animal is aware it is about to die, fear spurts its juices in the muscles. The meat darkens with knowledge. The cells contract. Music can lull an animal, soothe it; the blow comes but has to slice through a trance. You can stare through the cellophane at a steak and wonder if it was frightened when it got killed. Darkness cuts through the grain. People taste toughness and can't say where it's from. You probably have plenty besetting you without worrying if your dinner got a serenade. But what if you felt you were eating a serenade in a body, and wouldn't that pile song upon song inside of you, so at the hour of your death you might combat your own dark-cutting?

I attempted an easy version of Bach's *Chaconne in D-Minor*, the last movement, as the cows were herded down the chute of fences, marching into what looked like an airplane hangar. I was entranced by Brian McClintock, who seemed twice my height along with being twice my age, because he'd arrive to listen as my notes sailed over the lowing of the cows. Eyes like pinches of sky, I adored that, too, the wet entryways he had when he watched over me. He owned a ranch, but it was to raise bees; he made a living bottling and shipping honey. His workers cooked up exotic flavors, blueberry, guava. But the pure clover brand was famous; I used to imagine music tenderizing his hives until the comb oozed with—what's beyond famous? What's past everyone dying for a taste of you? Whenever I played Bartok, Brian said, "Faye, you're doing one half of a duet and then the other; that's amazing and sad." He knew music. He knew that sound finds a wave and holds on, and if it shatters the pieces of it fasten to other waves and ride farther over wider space.

Why did my father shoot my mother? The only clue Tia Clara offered was "You can figure out anything if your mind is dirty enough."

She'd drive off in her Impala to her job as a waitress at the Happy

Clam in Monterey, and she'd race home swathed in ocean air so visibly white her car looked wrapped in waxed paper. The artichoke fields bled altogether green, except where purple hairy thatches stuck out of the ones the pickers missed, the ones growing old; sometimes they dried up completely. You'd find them shrunken to a monkey's paw, like the kind the stories say grant three wishes.

One day I was lost in a Brahms lullaby, a blessing, but a cow turned and looked at me squarely. And I stopped, scared. It had entered the collective bovine consciousness that music could signal danger; the animals had learned a thing or two somehow and would now be passing it on to their unborn.

I turned twenty and was still a virgin. I became a mirror replica of my mother, with her green eyes and fair skin with an eerie resistance to burning, maybe because she and my aunt had grown up in the Azores, and the heavens so often filtered there through a fog. The newspaper photos of my father before he was sent to Folsom disturbed my theory that he was not my real father: I'd never seen him up close, but his face looked like a holograph stuck as a vapor to mine.

What kept me from evaporating was Brian staring at me, everywhere: he was forty-three and maybe didn't realize I was grown now, merely waiting for him to be done with one girlfriend after another.

I took a job as a nurse for Evan Redken, dying of lung cancer, rich enough to have a hospital bed at home and a morphine drip. He was a widower, childless. One Halloween at the cannery he owned, he presented a thousand-dollar check to everyone wearing a costume. He paid a needy farmer seven hundred dollars to purge his library of silverfish. He wore fedoras and pocket watches. He lay in bed with his skin broken out like a teenager's. The first thing I did was trim his white mustache because he always kept it neat, and he grasped my hand and murmured, as if he were bowing to me after the honor of a fox-trot, "Thank you, Miss Faye Silva." I had taken my aunt's surname. My father came from a dairy family called McSweeney.

I cooked for him and brought him a bedpan when he couldn't put off needing one any longer, and I waited behind a Japanese screen with cranes until he apologized for hiring me to empty it. Mostly what I did was read to him, sitting in a chair with taloned feet at his bedside. Sometimes when he slept I held his hand on the arm not attached to the drip.

One afternoon Mr. Redken asked if I'd heard of the Mandarin Question.

"Tell me," I said. I put down his copy of *Paradise Lost.*

He said it was an old philosophical puzzle. It went like this: if by ringing a bell at your side you caused the death of a mandarin in distant China whose vast fortune would then magically appear in your possession—and if you had never met this man and if it were guaranteed no one would ever be the wiser—*would you do it?*

"No," I said.

"The honest reply is something fuller than a yes or a no," he said. "You might be saying 'no' so that I'll think well of you." His eye sockets looked as if eggcups had been installed within his cranium, and the eyes had been cracked into the hollows. What if, he went on, I might, for instance, help him die by opening the valve in the drip and giving him some pills? He was scared to do it alone—what if I were told that part of his money would go to me?

"No," I said. "Did you say the deal is no one would know? The dead watching me would know. That means you'd know, and you're not nothing. I'd live knowing what I'd done, too. That means there'd be at least two of us."

He said, "How wise of you and how kind. For a moment, I can imagine I'm not dying alone. You'll remember that you make me want to hang on a bit longer."

I promised I'd stay with him. I adjusted a photo of his wife, Martha, so he could glimpse her across the room. When I stretched out on the covers alongside him, he jolted away and said he was a gentleman, and I said it was only that I would keep my arms around him. I owed someone that. He dozed and his breath stroked my face until daylight; I rose and went outside. I placed my hands on his stucco walls, the roughness and bumps like his ravaged skin. I soothed them, although of course they stayed the same, because even his house loved him so much it wanted to suffer as he did.

A doctor pronounced his cancer in full remission three weeks later. They took X-rays of Evan's lungs to use in medical textbooks. That is when I knew prayer to be a thing that is felt and not a system of requests, a thing of Light and Wave the way Music is Sound and Shape far past death. That is when I knew that everyone is a child of mine.

But also, I could not help myself entirely, the miracle got me wild, as if everyone would punch each other out for who'd get to touch me first. I got as far as Brian's apiary, ready to pitch myself at him and say the next life I needed to save was my own. A swarm burst out of a hive. The bees plunged their stingers into me, face and arms, and a few dove beneath my clothing and broke off their lower bodies in my skin.

I ran home screaming. Tia Clara dabbed calamine on the sores and said, "Serves you right."

I yelled that Brian was going to take me from her. He looked at me in a way that told me so. He smelled like the outdoors, large, blond, capable. He'd be able to carry me up a flight of stairs.

Aw, baby, he's beside himself because every day you look more like your mother. You think because she was forty-three when she was pregnant with you she wasn't after a young guy? He was so crazy about her he couldn't stay off her. I've kept you from the rumors.

I asked if he was my father.

No. He met her when she was pregnant. That's what set your father off, being older himself and finally having a family and thinking it would get taken from him.

Dinner that night was Dover sole. I held a raw fillet on my hand and delicate as it was, its spine missing but with a purplish fanning of lines on its back, it was my mother. Ghosts get pictured as milk-

and-smoke replicas of a body, but my mother had always been for me a suddenness of an object, the green snap on the horizon when the sunset's yoke pours out. Once she was a filter of lavender that dropped out of nowhere over a tractor, once she was a twist of algae, waving. My aunt yelled, "She was selfish. She drank like a fish, she was crazy for men, she wore shiny black high heels around the house."

She's a convex curve of air over a man even now.

Did I want to hear how my mother destroyed everyone who cared for her? After she died Brian took a job with the UN and was sent to Kenya. Far away, with wild animals roaming. But he lived in a hotel, took a bus to the compound where he taught English, wasn't allowed to wander. One square attached to another square, corridor, cage, never any relief from who you're stuck being.

That night in my bed, where a bee had pierced its sword below my breast, I scratched until the welt looked like that magic third nipple the Chinese say brings luck. Churning inside my mother, inhaling through a tube, I'd listened to a moan in her ear traveling down to flare inside mine.

Mr. Redken surprised me with a huge check because he swore I'd healed him. I bought a small boxy place for myself, and to my shock, Tia Clara said it was time, she'd try to be happy, I was ash slipping through her fingers.

The nuns used to warn, *Careful when your prayers are answered, nothing will be fixed, nothing will console you except what you have yet to grasp.*

I filled my afternoons at the Monterey Bay Aquarium. The jellyfish looked like fuchsias cut loose, dreamt big, blowsy. As a girl I'd pulled out the rods stuck up the skirts of the dancing-girl fuchsias to get the drop of honey inside. The peach domes of the jellyfish squeezed but never quite gripped the red tails billowing down from their middles. I lightly touched the glass as the moon-jellies fluttered with an ache from all the strings hanging out of them.

A young man sidled next to me and whispered, "You come here just like me." His reddish hair was cut short; he was tall. He was a soldier home from Iraq. His pupils put me in mind of those Easter eggs you peek inside, but instead of a hen and a farmhouse with a tiny heart for a chimney, I saw cinders, black jam, teeth. His tanned skin seemed cut shy of fitting his frame and then stretched over him. He held out an iPod, like a white wallet containing all the music he liked, there on his palm. He introduced himself as Henry Dunne.

I ran from him. I didn't want my first love to be someone come back from the dead; I'm sick of them, I've had it.

He caught up to me on Cannery Row and we ate dinner by the wharf. I told him my history. I said someone sweet once taught me that answering the Mandarin Question was a test of who someone was in this world and how he'd be in the next, and if he'd cherish you whether you were visible or invisible, and if he'd *care* if you had no *fucking* idea how to be *close* to anyone at all.

"Go on," said Henry.

I asked if he'd ring the bell that would kill the faraway mandarin if no one would be the wiser. Would he decide to become rich on death?

On the goose-barnacled pilings below us, water lapped as we passed the restaurants and shops. Henry did not speak until we were staring through the glass of a nightclub where people were drinking martinis. He said, "They're bell-ringers. We're all bell-ringers." He had a gutful of learning that we kill at a distance so that the wealth of the world appears magically at our feet, except it isn't one fabulous mandarin dying, it's thousands of the un-mandarins. Look under that strobe light. People are skulls with a sort of throbbing paper covering them, plus skeletons with expensive clothing.

"Well," I said, panicking again. "Don't you have a pretty view."

"My view is stunning," said Henry, kissing my face. "I'm looking at you."

In my empty home I came all to pieces in his arms and he did in mine, and then we pasted the both of us back together to form one porcelain urn. He was naked in my bed, shot with mottled shadow, and I was naked, too. He saw my violin and asked for some music. The moon tossed a disc of itself onto the floor, as if a child had cut it out of tissue. Below my feet the moon-tissue sprang alive, into a manta ray, pinned down but fluttering in one place.

I played a sure-fire old number, "Moon River." Henry was half covered with a sheet, and he was near crying. He said there are two types of people these days, ones who've been spit out the other side of violence and understand what it means to say *Never let me go,* and those who never think about the need to look for grace. His whiskers removed the top layer of some of my skin, and the air rushed in to heal the new layer coming through.

This is why we close our eyes while kissing: we instantly need to brand certain close-ups onto the underside of our eyelids. We need certain portraits to burn and flash whenever we blink when we're alone. I put down my violin and stayed where he could hold me fiercely, where I could feel my notes imbedded within him, cutting through the terror binding and darkening his muscles. Out of his insides there came a glowing, light as the touch of a newborn, come back to life to love me.

Lisbon Story

I opened the door to my father's apartment in the Campo de Ourique district of Lisbon—he'd sent me to sell it quickly before he died—and even before my eyes adjusted to the dark, I could feel that a stranger was lying in the bed. I froze in the hallway. He seemed thin and long but heaped, a tangle of cords more than a body. I jostled my suitcase, but he didn't stir. I inhaled the scent of what might be the corpse of a drug addict who'd wandered here from the Cais do Sodré station and persuaded the excruciatingly bribable *porteira* downstairs to let him expire in some warmth.

As always in Lisbon, my heart throbbed semaphores to call Tónio. That's all it ever takes for him to gather that I'm in town, but I'd also taken the precaution of sending a letter asking him to try some advance work toward the sale. He's an orbiter, an arranger, a whisperer in kings' ears, though what he actually does for a living, like many of the refugees from Angola, is construction work. He'd written back that he'd tracked down a possible buyer . . . though (*Ai, querida, you know the story here*) there were a few complications, which he'd save for my arrival.

I touched my way into the small, narrow kitchen, where I snapped on the light. The tiled picture of a caravel was tilted; a knife black with jam was tipping the bark canoe of a cheese rind on the cutting board. While I was grimacing at a cleaned-out tin of sausages, a young man wrapped in a sheet appeared in the doorway.

I shrieked—one of those girlish but full rending affairs.

Inside the V where he clutched the bed sheet, his chest revealed enough of his ribs to suggest the inner planks of a one-man fishing boat. His eyes were clouded but bright, beaming a child's buoyancy toward sickness.

My brain switched to Portuguese; I stammered that he could call me Catarina, and I sketched the outline of why this place was getting hurried to market . . . and was he perhaps a friend of António Magalhães? Was he the buyer for my father's apartment?

His name was Mateus Soares, and he spoke somewhat the English from watching many movie programs on the television set. He pointed a finger at me and said, "Bang, bang, especially your westerns." Toninho was a friend, yes, but as for owning a genuine roof over his head, no, ha ha and again ha ha, he barely had money for a dinner of pork fat.

"Well, now," I said. "How about if you go into the other room, and we can talk? You can explain where you belong, how's that sound?"

His answer was for his legs to buckle. He stayed kneeling, gripping the doorframe. He was wearing my ex-husband's sweatpants. Water began to gush from his skull.

When I'd tucked him back in the gray wet bed, I whispered, "*Tens SIDA, Mateus?*" The room smelled of spilled intestines.

He nodded. His eyes flickered, as if fireflies had stepped in the quicksand of his irises and were pulsating ferociously before they went under.

What had possessed me long ago to paint the bedroom the shade of a toy pig? Now that it had faded to a hybrid rose, the furnishings—rickety iron bed, splintery armoire, beige hooked rug, and spindly dresser—suggested probing insects resting indefinitely inside a flower.

"Let's see what you've hidden in this mess to feast on," I said.

I'd come to esteem Lisbon as a refuge after college and still loved to escape here. The narrow, tiled staircases edged with plants, the shirts with extended empty arms flapping in the breeze along the lines, balconies where no one appears: Lisbon rises before me as real as a dream printed out of my brain. I kept lots of provisions on hand so that I'd enter, after a lengthy absence, into a well-stocked home, but almost everything had been eaten. The cupboards, canary-yellow and apple-red, cheery plastics I'd installed in the postrevolutionary seventies, offered a lone tin of tomato soup that I brought to lukewarm. The freezer was empty except for a heel of bread.

I sat on the edge of the bed to feed Mateus. I was wearing a black skirt, white blouse, and lilac pumps—only British tourists wore sensible shoes—that kicked at his splay on the floor of magazines on American basketball. The pages exposed unearthly jumps and skeins of muscle. The dryness of his hand scraping mine alarmed me: a husk of a dead starfish. He grabbed the spoon and, smiling, splashed at the red pool in the dish in mock complaint and said, "You serve me the food of jails."

"My father was in a jail in this country, and trust me, he never got anything this good," I said.

"Your father is a criminal?" Thrilled, eager, he flopped toward me.

"No. No, you might say he's the opposite of a criminal." I eased backward.

"I don't understand, pretty little girl." *Menina bonitinha.*

"Don't call me that. I'm forty-five years old. *Jesus.*"

We stared at the room's sole attempt at decoration, Dad's framed poster of Wales, my mother's birthplace. He'd been born in northern Portugal and met my mother after his release from prison. She'd been on holiday in Lisbon and found it touching that he acted unstrung while riding in the funicular. They'd bought this place to live in as newlyweds awaiting their immigration papers to California, and they'd kept the property but never returned. He'd asked me to leave the map on display, so that Mama's ghost could visit if she liked.

Came a small voice from the bed: "I meant you are pleasing with the long dark hair and green eyes and your smallness."

"Don't say that either."

"My mother, she owns the green eyes." His voice spooled out the scratchy tape of his story. She was Lisboan and his father was Mozambican, and they lived by the Museum of Costumes and did not approve of him. He was only thirty-three. His boyfriend had thrown him out when he got ill.

I murmured about his bad luck. I was sorry.

He quoted a Portuguese line about destiny: If shit were worth money, the poor wouldn't have assholes.

Mateus could easily be one of Tónio's lovers; he was forever breaking up with one man or another, though he'd sobbed terribly over a guitarist from Cabo Verde. Beyond the rattling pane, Lisbon was coming to, the trucks grinding and trolley wires singing that pitch best heard by animals, while the Christmas lights—in tints from eggshell to vanilla, strung as bells and holly—buzzed in their sockets over the streets.

I repeated that my father was dying of stomach cancer in California, and letting go of this perch was his last unfinished business. He wanted to survive long enough to sell his spot here and divide the profit among his three grandchildren, my brother David's three.

"I cannot buy nothing," said Mateus.

Right. Quite so. I'd help him get into a hospice that dealt with AIDS patients—wasn't it good to be in a country with socialized medicine?—because I had another sick man to put at peace.

"Ai, no," he said, turning over to face away from me. "My desire now is to die in a nice house. I am not going to no hospital."

Americans solve their problems by fleeing. From the hallway I left a message on Tónio's phone machine to meet me at once at the Santa Apolónia station. I trusted my voice to find him immediately and have him plain materialize. I abandoned my luggage and, without saying good-bye, raced the four flights down and stood on Rua Carlos da Maia to stare at the ground-floor windows and shut curtains of Deolinda Simões, the porteira, the gorgon at the gate. My father never failed to mail her checks to watch his property, though we were sure she rented it out on her own and pocketed the cash and, up until now, managed to spirit her renters into some fissure if my brother or I planned to visit.

I bolted over the dragon's-tooth mosaic sidewalks, past the Chinese restaurant run by immigrants from Macau, and hurried to the taxi queue on the Rua Ferreira Borges. My cabdriver inquired if I was about to become ill, did I need help? I was hoping I looked merely deep in prayer. My hands were sealed over my eyes as we climbed the Calçada da Estrela, where the cobalt and turquoise tiles gleamed on the shops stocked with King's cakes, glacéed citron, baskets spilling pineapples from Madeira, and port bottles with chalky stenciling to show their age. The cable on the Prazeres streetcar ahead of us fell from the overhead wires, and my driver, grizzled as scraped toast, slammed on the brakes but hummed a sweet, broken tune. When the streetcar jolted forward, its cable like a femur bouncing on the wire, we tore east along the waterfront and I almost catapulted through the windshield from the force of his stop at Santa Apolónia.

On a plate-glass window looking into the station's waiting room, my reflection was smeared, as if I'd thrown my face to splatter on a mirror. Ostensibly my father wished to spare me the trauma of prolonged deathbed scenes; he intended to go to his Maker in a pine-scoured room with trained caretakers. He'd been fond of his forty years as a nurse at Children's Hospital and regretted that he couldn't die with their teddy-bear wallpaper as a backdrop to David and me. But the other reason for packing me off to Lisbon was that the year before his cancer was diagnosed I'd imploded into jigsaw pieces after my husband, James, blurted that I "represented confinement." I was, with unforgivable timing, my father's last nursing project; childless and solitary since my divorce, I was going to send him worrying into the other world.

I scanned the crowds, anxious for them to present me with Tónio. The Tejo across the road lapped against the hulls of boats, an incoherent lullaby. Toninho! There you are! Tónio Magalhães! Grinning at me from the opposite side of the Marginal. Wearing broth-colored khakis and a blue-striped shirt, a vastly different getup from the one he'd been sporting when we'd first met twenty years ago. I'd been walking down the Avenida da Liberdade when an African in a bell-bottomed, chartreuse tie-dyed pantsuit pinched the back of my calf and said, "You are the first white girl in this city I have made smile." He later denied that he ever wore such an outfit.

He tapped with a what-goes-on-in-that-mind-of-yours briskness at his temple to convey, *You said the* south *side of the highway, minha sempre-perdida Catarina!* He looked gaunt, but then he was lamppost-tall, and perhaps his habit of manifesting out of nowhere suggested the notion of the spectral.

I barely missed getting hit by a car as—horns blaring—I dashed through the traffic into his arms. "My God," he said, "you almost got yourself killed and then I'd have to die, too!" My hand on the giant rosary-bead decades of his spine. His scent was of Mustela oil, like a pressing of hazelnuts and lab-invented musk, and we were of a perfect mismatch of height for him to settle his head on top of mine. Though we often sleep side by side, we'd never tangled in the ruinous desperation of love that leaves no one standing.

"Cat, I am so sick, oh my Lord, about your father."

The sun scorched off my corneas, broke the membrane sealing in the water, as if it were only simple, physical laws that had me crying.

Ai, Catarina. Não chores como chuva. He cradled my head against his chest. My father used that expression: Don't cry like rain. When the sorrow bursts out of you as a visible storm.

"Honey pie," he said. *Unny-pah.* He'd picked the word up from the fifties sitcoms hailed down into his war-pounded Luanda. He tossed it at me often enough, but it never failed to crack me up.

"You need to tell me everything, Senhor T," I said.

"Honey pie, I must sit down. *You* want to sit down, too, believe me, Catarina."

We found a green bench with a view of the dock. Discarded napkins from a stand selling lemon squash and coconut tarts scuttled like albino crabs around our ankles. He was mottled with sweat as he took my hand in his and said, "Your father is not the only one to possess that apartment, I am sorry."

"He's owned that place for sixty years. I sent you a copy of the deed."

"Honey pie, I discovered that after the revolution some *grande queijo* in the Communist Party said, 'OK, I am making a new deed, I own it, not some American who doesn't live here anymore, it's mine.'"

"If someone else stole it, why hasn't he ever tried to move in?"

"Because he died a few weeks after making the false deed. I found it when I was nosing around the Associação Lisbonense de Proprietários, and when I tried to track him down I met his widow. She was in the dark about it. When I showed her your father's deed and said the place was for sale and I hoped she wouldn't try anything ridiculous, she said that she hated all Communists, including her dead husband, and she wants to buy an apartment for her granddaughter. She'll pay your asking price. António Magalhães forever at your service, Cat-Cat."

"So why do you look as if you've swallowed a bucket of nails?"

Ah. Just one slight problem. Mateus.

"I was once insane about him, honey pie. We were never lovers. Even dying, the bastard knows I worshipped him and will do as he asks. I paid your porteira to let him stay. The one little catch is that the widow who wants to buy is superstitious; she refuses to make a transaction while a dead man is in residence. She thinks it is more with the grace to let my friend be there to his end before the sale begins, so that he does not feel rushed, with the roof being transferred from him, if that is his final wish with God."

"*His* wish? Mateus—I'm sorry for him, I am—but he can go to a hospital, and this woman can lose her voodoo hang-up and sign a check, and then I can go home to my father. Whose last wish includes cleaning up his affairs here. By me. For *his* grandchildren. This is *absurd*."

"Yes, of course it is. But you're here to sell it, querida, yes? You asked me to wave my magic wand and help. I thought you'd be glad for a buyer this fast. Fast . . . with a small delay so that Mateus—"

"Mateus can go stay with you. Since you're so in lo-ove with him."

"He wishes to approach his death in a pleasant home. You are aware, honey pie, that my flat is a shit-hole. I am the wizard with arrangements for everyone but myself, as you have pointed out a few times. Also, and perhaps I am handing you the gun to shoot at me with, but his parents have said they will take him in, but they do not like him. His mother will read to him from the Bible with the parts underlined about the sodomy, and that is to go to the other world with a nightmare in the ear and in the eye and right up the ass. No good."

"You had *no right* to move your *friend* in. There's no *time* to fuck around."

"Your father can go to his rest, and may God bless him very much, knowing a finish to his business in Lisbon is near, while another dying man—"

He caught my arm as I seized my purse to leave. He'd used the words "father" and "dying" in the same sentence.

"Cat, I'm so sorry, don't cry," he said, tightening his grip on me. "Please. Don't run away. We're fighting like tired married people. We get so much almost right."

Seagulls wheeled and cawed and plunged into the river. I collapsed back onto the bench and said, "T, tell me this isn't some assisted suicide thing."

"OK, he did ask me that. But baby, you know me, I told him I could not kill anyone. He agrees to stay until he is so bad he won't know where he is, and then I'll take him to the hospital. Don't you see, honey pie? It is a chance for me to tend the passage of someone in a good way. Plus the sale is for sure, God willing. Maybe God prefers that your father not watch his place in Lisbon go away in his lifetime."

"You're making me crazy, T."

He put his arm around me and said, "I forget your father is American and you people think that things get finished. I wanted to buy time and make everybody happy. But OK, it is my job now to take care of you. I'll tell Mateus to go to his parents."

The roof of the daylight sky rippled early to let the sharp stars streak down as tinsel pooling around our feet. We were wading forward, with the world shrunk to an arcade with its top and walls draped with people and buildings and newsstands and here and there a fresco curve of sky. Sometimes a few flowers. Chatter and, from somewhere, a moan going toward diminuendo. We passed a contingent of young women wearing belts that wrapped around and stuck out the back loop of their trousers. Some American imports had once flooded in, and everyone figured this must be the style; who could have waists so large? A model was being photographed against a white stucco wall and I stepped into the road for a closer look: her skin and hair were damp and she seemed naked under a tease of a lime-colored raincoat. I did not detect the Prazeres streetcar bearing down on me until Tónio threw me onto the sidewalk and from there I saw the aghast face of the conductor gliding toward the cemetery at the end of the line, his hand still blasting the horn. Cemitério dos Prazeres, the Cemetery of Pleasures. Did that mean that earthly pleasure was strong enough to continue past death? Or that death brought heavenly pleasure? "That streetcar almost killed you," said Tónio. "Jesus and Ma*don*na, Cat."

Tónio's arm stayed fixed around me as we barged into a piano melody filling my father's apartment. Rachmaninoff. Blaring.

Mateus was sitting in bed with the sheet tented over his knees and, in the way that presence speaks to presence, he sensed that Tónio had given him up. His wailing caused Tónio to cross the room, where Mateus clung to him like a frightened child, and drove me into the living room, where I picked up the plastic cassette holder. It belonged to Mateus; maybe he'd bought it from the transients who hawked music outside the train station. It certainly did not belong to my father or to me.

Tónio was chanting, *No, it's not her fault. Pá, it's time to be a son again for your parents, you must tell them good-bye.*

The living room was as motley as the rest of the place; it retained its original wallpaper with violet sprigs, an *oratório* to Saint Anthony, and a cabinet my parents had filled to bursting with tableaux of miniatures, Russian dolls, toy soldiers, farm beasts, and enameled and ceramic figurines. I'd added a rug busy as a tapestry and an incongruous oak dining set. A nearly blind great-aunt had passed her gentle widowhood here, and I needed only to stroke the furniture to absorb the heat left behind by the wandering pads of her fingertips. I parked myself on the sofa, which was upholstered in a print of stylized compass roses that wear and blur had changed into blastulae.

Look, brother, I spoke out of turn, Catarina's here so end of story, OK, pá? . . . go home where they love you, of course they do, shh, pá . . .

The piano music was helping drown out their voices, but it was also making me as queasy as it always used to make my father. He'd spent a lifetime trying to hide this from me, but once, at the Guerreros' Christmas party, when I was ten, I watched him brace himself against a wall while someone thumped carols on the Steinway. I asked my mother why he'd gone home ahead of us, complaining of nausea.

It took another week before my mother broke her promise to my father never to tell me that when he'd been young in a village up north, he'd been required to play the piano loudly enough to cover the screams of the men being tortured in the makeshift jail during the fascist regime. Mother was big-boned, fair but jet-haired, a pragmatist; she'd been a vet's assistant in Wales and then in California, and dispensing the truth about animals had tempered her quiet tone into the straightforward.

My father's original career had been as a journalist. The trouble broke when he wrote a newspaper article scolding the government for not providing better medicine for the poor. On the same page as his editorial, some other newsman—or a shaving of metal fallen onto the printing press—had altered the line "Rare men run this country" to "Rat men run this country." *Ratos* instead of *Raros*. (I learned on my own that *rata* was also slang for cunt.)

The editor was exiled to Galicia, no one confessed to the alteration, and my father was arrested at the house he shared with his elderly parents and brothers. The soldiers explained that his job now was to entertain them with his musical talent.

He was a decent player, nothing special. The piano was a moldering upright in a corner of a drafty edifice serving as a jail, and the screams from someone invisible in the depths pierced him. The notes he hit muffled the sounds before they swept down into the valley.

He quit playing.

They said, Keep going or we'll chop off a finger.

He did not attempt Debussy; too airy. Liszt would be better. Liszt ranges over the keyboard, gets showy, never settles down.

The screams escalated. A man emptying himself out.

My father dropped his hands into his lap, and a boy in a uniform several sizes too large raised a knife and, at a slant, sliced the fat pad off my dad's wedding-ring finger. The miniscule chopped part would heal, but it would remain a flat, dead spot.

My father managed scales until his blood streaked the keys. The shrieks turned into primitive gasping, hitting a crescendo. Once again my father wrapped his notes around the noise. Then he took his hands off the keys yellowed as bad teeth and said, Cut off my head. Do it fast. I quit.

The unseen man was delivering staccato, roof-lifting, gut-contorting calls. Then the sound stopped cold. My father gaped through the window at the beige fields and waited for the torture of the man in the back room to continue, but there was only a quiet of epic, multiplying shape.

My mother said that it was utterly impossible to gauge whether the man in the back room had been killed, or dragged off, or—this was the guess she imbedded in herself as true in order to convince my father it was true—someone had been deliberately hollering to frighten him as his punishment before he got shipped out to a year of solitary confinement.

Mateus was lightening up on his infernal crying, subsiding into gulping and choking. I snapped off the music and pitched myself at the telephone.

I started out wanting merely to report to my father that we'd found a buyer, but he snatched up his receiver before the end of the first ring as though he'd been waiting at the ready, and before I could speak I heard, "Catarina, there are problems, naturally. Tell me." I didn't get far past explaining about Communist leaders and the superstitions of their widows and delays when I blurted about a man in the house. Sick. No, dying. AIDS. Displaced. African, sort of. Would my father please calm him down, since he had a lifetime of speaking to patients in their beds, persuade him that it was time to leave? He had parents willing to take him in, though he was estranged from them.

My father would be sitting in the velour chair worn down to its shining warp. Even at eighty-five he looked remarkably like James Joyce: trim, nearsighted, cerebral, and given to bowties. The carpeting was a cornflower tint, and geodes caught sunrays on a mantel that had been barnacled with them since my childhood. His feet would be on the footstool I'd done in needlepoint the summer my mother died of breast cancer; I'd stitched a pride of lions with manes of orange tendrils.

"Put him on." He sighed with enough force for his words to billow out of the phone as a mist that dampened my ear. I pictured the fog that continually wraps pieces of San Francisco as if they're ornaments to be swathed and shipped.

I signaled for Tónio to pick up the line in the bedroom while I unplugged the phone in the living room and found the jack in the hallway. When I sat on the bedroom floor to listen in, Mateus and my father, who'd lived in California over half a century but remained instinctively Lusitanian, were fording that tributary-rich stream of politeness that must precede diving into business. Mateus, now dry-eyed, assumed the pose of a teenager set for a lengthy gossip, head propped on pillows. . . . *if it might be acceptable to speak cordially with thee, esteemed owner . . . and before I might trouble you regarding my home, in which you are presently lodged, I should inquire as to your profession . . .*

"I used to be a fry-cook at Café Nicola," said Mateus. "It is an art of timing, pá."

"You are possibly aware, my friend, that the Japanese word *tempura* comes from the Portuguese word for *time,* and from the Portuguese teaching them about the right timing and degree of heat for frying." My father had a habit of figuring that exchanging colorful facts sufficed as intimacy with strangers.

"Imperialists, pá."

Tónio was on a chair by the bed; he bent in two, his elbows on his knees, and his head plummeted into his hands.

"Excuse me?"

"Missionary imperialists in Asia. In Africa. You white people should stay home, pá."

Senhor T's head sunk lower, as if something very interesting had materialized on the floor.

"Young man, that's a funny thing to say. Since right now, as I understand it, you're in my home."

"Dad?" I said. "Listen. I'll figure this out. I'm sorry I called."

"You're dead, I'm dead, it doesn't matter who goes first, pá."

"You keep calling me Father. As your father, more or less, I'm wondering if you might remove the rudeness from your tone."

"Father? You're not my father," said Mateus. "My father is a God-fearing son of a bitch who despises me. He is dead to me."

"Dad, he's not saying 'pai,' he's saying 'pá.'"

"Pá. He's saying 'pá.' What does that mean?"

"Pal, man, guy. It's every other word here now."

"How delightful. My beautiful language mutilated. I'm not your 'pal.' You are in the place I plan to give to my grandchildren."

"Your imperialist grandchildren can go to the devil, pá."

Tónio stood and pressed a hand on Mateus's forehead, aiming to push the fury back inside him or at least pin it in one spot.

"*Credo.*" The word means "I believe," but when stretched to contain ten Es, it means *I do not believe this!* My father was aiming for thirty Es.

I set the phone on the floor, where sound buzzed around the edges of the receiver. Mateus lapsed into a fast slang I couldn't follow. Tónio snapped on the small television on the dresser and returned to stroking Mateus's head until the venom seemed to retract. When I retrieved the phone my father was sputtering.

"Catarina, what's that racket?"

"There's something called the Ducky Song that comes on the TV to send the children to bed. I guess it soothes him."

My father considered television a sinister drug. He hadn't been allowed to silence it in the large ward at Children's Hospital, so he'd arranged a card table to show how to fold origami. One victorious night, all the patients gave up television to shape giraffes, pelicans, and many-sided stars.

Mateus slammed down his phone to attend to the ducks.

"I'm still here, Dad."

"They need ducks to tell them to go to bed. Don't children there ask their fathers for a night blessing anymore?"

"It's a catchy tune," I told him. "The cartoon ducks play xylophones. The problem is the music gets stuck in your head." I'd started despising his night blessing when I was fourteen. He'd make the sign of the cross over me and ask God in Portuguese to make me a big saint. When he'd borne enough of my complaining, he remarked that perhaps I'd become too mature for this kind of good night.

The cord was long enough for me to hide in the hallway. "Dad, Tónio is here, too. He's trying to talk Mateus into going home. Then we can proceed. With the sale. It's all so ridiculous, but I don't think I can handle calling in the white coats to have him forcibly removed."

"No, no, don't do that to someone who's sick. No."

"I could find out who else is out there, on the market. I could find someone this afternoon. Or it could take months, Dad. Longer."

"I like that the buyer will be a woman putting her husband's theft to right. Erasing a sin is good, even if it isn't yours. Even if the harm never came into view. Listen. I'm proud of you."

"Good night, Dad. Daddy? I'll be home soon."

Tónio had finished delivering Mateus to his rest and was unrolling a sleeping bag for me in the living room. I climbed into it. He collapsed next to me on a nest of blankets.

"I'm such a coward, honey pie."

"You're not a coward. How are you a coward?"

He said that Mateus wanted to pretend he lived in his own grown-up home before he left the earth. Perhaps he should have helped him die with that vision intact.

"Tónio, I've read those Hemlock Society things. You have to put a plastic bag over the person's head to make sure he's dead."

"This is about giving a man his last wish."

"I know," I said, sharply. "That's why I'm here, remember?"

In the cabinet filled with miniatures, ceramic bluebirds in a disheveled, merry row were playing ceramic instruments. I'd never noticed that in the dark the dots of violets on the wallpaper, and the amber drips from the sweating of the glue and aging of the print, formed a halo of quarter and whole notes around the outside of the cabinet. Tónio burrowed down so his head fit against my breast. I said, "I don't mean to bark at you, T. What did you love about him?"

"He was a genius of a cook. His timing, it's a gift. He snuck into the Nicola to cook a fish for himself and steal it. But he said he fell in love with standing there waiting for the fish to get done. I liked that. But the real reason I fell for him is his singing voice. He can go over high C. Can you believe it? A voice that deep. Where does it come from? It's like he doesn't produce it himself, he offers a place for a sound above high C to hide. But I could not bear waiting for him to be done with one person and then another, it was too much like watching myself, and I became the one he'd come crying to when something ended." He fidgeted on the floor, his elbow barely missing my face. "Honey pie, I cannot sleep with that looking at us." He got up and closed the little doors of the oratório to Saint Anthony, my grandfather's wedding gift to my father and mother, on a lace runner on a side table. In the hollow in the chest of the wooden saint, under a thin glass pane, was a sliver of finger bone that was supposed to be from someone who'd touched the saint during his lifetime.

When he flung himself back down onto his bedding, he hooked a leg over me, and I said, "If he's shut in his coffin, Senhor T, you're stuck protecting me from the ghosts with their daggers and the screaming scary stuff."

He said I shouldn't imagine otherwise. Hadn't he always kept me safe and sound?

I stroked his blanketed leg. "Yes," I said, and that was enough for him to drop into an instant slumber. He'd forgotten that in my family "safe" and "sound" had never quite fit together. My ear rested as a stethoscope where T's heart pressed up to send a pulse through the side of my face. This must have eased me into some kind of rest, because when whimpering filled the air I sprang to attention in my sleeping bag, unsure where I was. Tónio stretched, half awake, and groaned, "I put him to bed, it's your turn."

With his head stuck below his pillow, Mateus looked like an ostrich, gawky. I removed the pillow. His hair looked singed, and I stroked the tufts of it and uttered that timeless night litany: *Do you need water? A story? Where does it hurt?* until I fathomed what he wanted: my hearing his calling out. My stroking his hair.

I'd slept in this room with Tónio our first night together, never undressing. It was more of a clutching, my astonished inspection of how thin he was, and his embrace of me at first was so ferocious I seemed to be underwater and breathing through a straw that pierced the surface. There was a package of condoms near expiration left over from a love affair with a fellow I broke into fragments over, but when I mentioned them, Tónio said, *I don't like you like that but, please, if you do not mind holding me.* The war in Angola had left him an orphan adrift, one of the earth's totally fucked. I quit my usual anxious wondering what was supposed to happen next, until I had a sense of being pressed whole to the inside of him, and I left that print of myself there for him to carry around, and his physical weight sank inside my ribs, where it expanded so he'd stay trapped in the barred cage of my chest. But I was aware that my arms were mine and his were his, and my legs belonged to me and his—his were so long the muscles seemed a topography rolling away. The light from the streetlamp outside exploited a weak horizon in the blinds so that it seemed to have hurled a knife in to cut the throat of Wales, but out of the slit spilled a brilliance. The plastic over the framed map had refracted this dazzling strip onto us, laying a cool cloth of light over both our foreheads.

I kissed Mateus's fevered temple. He had drifted away.

When I lay down next to Tónio he lifted a lock of my hair to fit behind my ear and said, "I wish I could desire you, you need so much."

"Go to sleep," I said. "Stay with me, Tónio. I love you to pieces."

But as he slumbered my own sleep was so fitful you'd have imagined I was choreographing abandoned sex with someone a movie studio still needed to superimpose on the film. I got up and peered through the window every hour. Night in Lisbon speckles itself blue, tosses sapphires onto black cloth. The sapphires dissolve by daybreak, but the sky keeps the saturation of the gems of the night in the same way that clear water, amassed, holds blue.

I came to with a start to find Tónio missing. The phone rang, and my father's panic trilled over the wire. "Catarina? I keep falling. This is going to be the first day I can't go see your mother." It was nighttime in California, predawn.

"Dad? Is David there? Call David to come take care of you."

My father—even when he was ill—visited my mother daily in her cerulean vase in the Columbarium, a minute's stroll from the scene of their married life on Arguello Boulevard. She awaited him in the niche they'd tiled with *azulejos* as their final home. One evening, after he'd again put on his suit and tie to go calling on her, I'd said, "Daddy, isn't it time to move on?" He'd tried to check the disappointment in me that made him tilt his head, as if he couldn't possibly have heard me correctly. "I was faithful to your mother," he'd said. "Why shouldn't I stay like that, especially since she's in a weakened state?"

"I'm coming home, Dad. Enough already."

"No. Something good and without death will arrive so the sale can happen. I can't guess what but I have faith. I'm a week away from the hospital. You can visit me there. I couldn't stomach my daughter hovering, bracing herself about taking me to the bathroom."

"Call David."

"I couldn't bear him hovering either. Is our patient surviving over there? Allow me to chat with my fellow countryman. I have a joke for him."

"A joke."

"Yes."

Tónio came in, carrying groceries. He set bottles of Luso water and Sumol pineapple seltzer on the kitchen counter and lingered in the doorway, watching me. He'd brought in the scent of the ocean. Fish.

He assisted me in performing the same fandango with the telephone lines so that I could listen as my father said to Mateus, "Young man? Good morning. Is it morning? In Lisbon? When I was a boy in Portugal, my father inflicted a joke on me to start every day."

This was news. The sepia photos of my *Vovô* with his scrub-brush mustache and crazed leopard's squint didn't suggest a laugh riot.

"What happens when five Portuguese people argue politics?"

Tónio was leaning against the armoire. In its oval mirror I could see the whorl at the back of his cropped hair, as if it's where the entirety of his body refuses to vanish despite being down his own drain.

Mateus said, "Wait, wait, wait. It's on the tip of my tongue."

The pregnant pause across the seas between Lisbon and San Francisco was interrupted by my father's ineptitude with comic timing. "They form seven political parties."

Mateus laughed. "That's it. Good one, pá. Are you buttering me up before you scream at me to leave?"

"I don't have the strength for the scream in me," said my father. "I was hoping you'd offer your personal assurance that the *ginjinha* shop is still open in the center of town. I've been wondering. My wife and I went there after we got married, to toast each other."

"You must not have had many friends, pá. It's the size of a closet."

"It was mostly the two of us, back then. Has it been torn down?"

I could have told him it was thriving, a pint-sized dispensary serving nothing but cherry liqueur on the Largo do São Domingos.

"It's always the same, pá," said Mateus. "Who knows how the owner survives."

My father said that the ache in him was awful. When he was much younger he'd drink some ginjinha whenever his system was upset. He filled Mateus's ear and mine with the war story of Monção: when the town was surrounded a woman scraped together the last of the flour to make two buns to throw at the enemy. The invaders withdrew, unnerved at the town's defiant wish to speed up hunger rather than surrender. He said he felt like that, under siege and pretending he wasn't starving.

"I'm starving. I can only swallow applesauce," he said. "Catarina, could I trouble you to stroll out for some ginjinha? It'll quiet me if you're drinking it. Buy some for our patient there, too."

"Why, thank you," said Mateus. He said he'd been craving something without knowing what. Cherries in firewater. Yes, good.

"Call me back and describe it," said my father. "Please."

"I think I can manage that," I said. "Good-bye, Daddy."

Tónio picked up a towel lying on the floor, blue with nearly scrubbed-away roses, and wiped Mateus's face. He lifted the towel and stared at its underside, as if expecting his friend to leave a veronica imprinted on the cloth. Then he studied Mateus, as if by chance he'd find, instead, the faintest outline of the dissolving roses on his face.

"Pá," said Mateus, and he gripped Toninho's arm, "I'm not sure why I always seem to get my way, but I've got nothing to show for it."

Toninho's face split open to spill out his radiance. "You fucking idiot," he said softly. "Nothing to show for it? You've got people here dancing for you, dancing around you, dancing—"

Mateus grinned. "OK, OK."

"Dancing off on an errand of mercy," I said from the doorway, trying to raise my tone into light animation. "Say thank you."

"Hurry back," he called out at me. I had to take him as boyish;

ill or not, he didn't come across as a man in his thirties and surely never had. "Thank you for hurrying," he said. It was the first time we were both smiling at precisely the same moment.

Tónio said he would cook an early lunch for the lord and master. I walked past the Pingo Doce—the Sweet Drop—grocery store, where pigs' heads hung on hooks, to be stewed for sausage for the holidays. My father had refused to take us to the *matanças* in the valley, because he said the squeal of the pigs when the knife came down was unearthly and no one who heard it could ever get rid of it.

Angels, droll and flirty, were stenciled around the entranceway of the ginjinha shop. Shallow shelves housed the liqueur, the bottles glowing crimson, like the blood of Saint Gennaro readying to bubble alive. The cherries swelling in a vat on the counter looked like the eyeballs of cows or a hen's painful laying of eggs. The owner and I commenced an argument about why he could sell me liqueur but not glasses to carry it. I offered to pay lavishly. His glower suggested his disapproval of foreigners who thought they could march in and make demands. He wasn't in the business of selling glassware; obviously I had mistaken his humble but dignified establishment for a kitchen-supply emporium. A fellow customer said, "She's the American girl who was on the television last year about her book. She's one of us, in a way." I'd taped a segment for my novel about a Portuguese nun. Television is one of the magic words of the universe. The owner frowned but gave me what I asked for.

I carried two glasses like chalices brimming garnet, toasting the streets. Here's to the gargoyles on cornices; here's to you, funiculars and iron Juliet balconies, and to you, azulejos—tiles of griffins, bears, and explorers in the hues of sky and ocean, cloud and whitecap.

The men were in the kitchen when I arrived, with the deep fryer on the stove. The fumes of the oil heating mixed with the boozy cherry aroma I brought in. Tónio was extracting *carapaus,* their eyes like cross-sections of marbles, from their waxy paper and dipping them in beaten egg and rolling them in cornmeal while Mateus was slumped on a chair, waiting for the oil to hit the proper temperature.

"Cheers," I said, handing a glass to Mateus, who downed it fast, and to Tónio, who snaked an arm through mine. From the center of the caduceus we made, he and I took turns drinking. T's Adam's apple pushed out and I brushed it with my fingertips and felt it jump as it got painted with alcohol.

"Stand back," said Mateus.

He got up from the chair and studied the cauldron of oil, took one of the fish by its tail, and plunged it mouth first into its bath below a rolling boil. Waiting with the scoop made of metal netting, he looked like a marionette with the strings cut, a dry creature glued to sticks. But happy somehow. In the pose of his element. He looked away from the cauldron, as if to show that he was not in a hurry.

He extracted the first carapau and Tónio said, "Perfect."

Mateus was elated. "Perfect to the end, pá."

The carapau looked as if it had tumbled in sand on the beach, and then it had flipped fore and aft in the sunlight until it was done. I said, "Unbelievable. Goodness." He nodded. A tremor almost dropped him to his knees, and I eased him into the chair near the stove. He needed to rest before doing the same for the other two fish.

I set the table in the living room with placemats from the Maritime Museum—prints of sea monsters on indigo—and found some pale orange tapers. Oscillating from the clotheslines of the buildings across the courtyard were vibrant linens, as if someone had savaged sky-sized bouquets, the petals stuck and writhing. Mateus said he was getting wobbly and would eat on the sofa. Tónio sliced up a pineapple.

We didn't speak as we admired the fish and the fruit and the teardrops of fire quivering in place on top of the candles.

That pause of beholding it all was our grace.

The air was drinking the vapors of brine from the fish. It had been drinking up some salting of the air for so many years here. This place could have been mine. But I'd told my father back when final promises needed to be made to give it to David's children. I had many friends I could stay with in Lisbon.

Soon that widow and her granddaughter might be doing nothing more than strolling through this room, suddenly at a loss. They'd tear the engorged salted air and there'd be a storm of weeping and it might frighten them, their inability to say where it came from.

"Amen," said Toninho. "Get out the shovels and begin to dig." We rattled our knives and banged our plates and lowered our heads and got to work.

Mateus said, "I believe someone is in need of calling the father, yes? Tell him the drink put a lamp in me." His hand rested on his gut.

I dialed California and said, "Dad? The cordial tastes like the inside of a cherry tree. Mateus says thanks. We're having a feast. Tónio cut up some pineapple. Mateus fried three carapaus."

"You can't find those here."

"I know." With Tónio pulling his earlobe in that universal signal of *This is so fine,* I tucked the phone where I could speak and listen and took up my fish knife again; I take pride in my Lusitanian skill at filleting a fish so that head and spine stay intact, and the skin, skimmed off whole, stays a flap that can be folded back to re-cover the fleshless place.

"Tell him the pineapple looks especially well presented," said Tónio.

"Dad? Our pineapple is that good miniature kind, deep yellow."

"How about the coffee?" he asked. "When I first left with your mother we searched for coffee like we had there."

"They import the coffee here from Brazil," I said.

"Africa," said Tónio.

"I miss the food," said my father.

"You're forgetting the people, Dad," I said.

"No, I haven't, not for a single minute. They're as gentle as God makes them."

Mateus leaned over and erupted in choking. His plate spilled off his lap and clattered onto the rug; his gnawed fish came to rest in a pear tree. His whooping noise settled into a gagging and he used up his strength to get to a sitting position, and Tónio leapt from his chair and pounded him on the back, but he couldn't fill his lungs. His eyes bulged at me. He raked his nails on a round ochre pillow.

"Dad, hold on, Mateus must have swallowed a fish bone."

With the phone pinned between my shoulder and ear, I got on one side of him and Toninho stayed on the other. Mateus's skinny arms were flailing; a curtain of scarlet rose below his skin.

"Catarina," said my father, composed. "I taught you the Heimlich. Put the phone down and try that."

Mateus was weightless enough for me to get behind him and brace my fists below his ribs while Tónio held him steady, and I banged upward. Nothing. I tried a few more times, my fists bashing so hard I was afraid of cracking something.

I grabbed the phone and yelled, "Dad? Dad? It's not working!"

"Be calm," he said. His words, as he spoke, had spaces between them. "Go into the kitchen and put on rubber gloves. Tónio's there?"

"Yes. Yes, yes."

"Put on your gloves, and have Tónio pry the patient's teeth apart and hold them open. Press his tongue down with a spoon. The bone's probably in his throat. Go on now."

I dashed into the kitchen and struggled as the gloves stuck, and when my fingers were in them Tónio yelled, "Christ!" because Mateus was going into spasms. The two men were wrapped up in a writhing way, with T's eyes lit as he looked at this convulsing kindling. I seized the phone and my dad said, "It's the last cat in the litter waiting to be born. Pull it out to save the mother. Go on."

I told T to pry open Mateus's teeth and keep them apart. Plying a fork because we hadn't put out spoons, I pressed the muscle of his tongue down with the tines. A pin-sized white object was down in his throat. I made a pass at pulling it out, but I only made him gag.

I snatched up the phone and shrieked, "Dad? Dad?"

And I went sheer blank for a second, the way we do when we wish ourselves far from where we are. Tónio came to my rescue by yanking the gloves off my hands hard enough for the phone with my father inside it to fall and hit my foot, a good rap that doubled me in two, so that, head lowered, I heard my father, as if he were shouting up from the earth, "*Know* you're going to save him! Now *do* it!"

Tónio heard him as well. I tilted back Mateus's head. Toninho was already wielding the fork while reaching past the wet rim of the dying man's mouth. Saliva pooled into the cavity. My forehead was against Toninho's and a last exhalation jet out of T's nostrils. I quit breathing, too. The phone spun around on the floor, as if it were a little boat with my father in it in a tiny whirlpool.

Tónio reached in for that infinitesimal swelling, the claw of an almost-newborn cat reaching the hook of itself upward, and the plastic of the glove gave him traction, and he pulled, and the bone slid out, along with the sloshing return of the feast, the contents of Mateus's gut. He tipped forward and vomited onto the shoreline where the oak planks of the floor met the medieval rug with its fruit trees and birds, and Tónio dropped the fish bone and rested his head on Mateus's back.

The bone was shorter than the length of my ring finger, only the width of a wire.

Tónio held a palm to Mateus's forehead and muttered, "I'm here, pá. I'm right here. It's over now."

We stretched Mateus flat on the sofa, and I groped around shaking to retrieve my father and said, "Dad, are you still there? We've got to clean him up but he's fine. I mean he's breathing." The stench of stomach juices was of the slaughterhouse, a blast of a carnal odor I knew from my relatives who were ranchers in the San Joaquin Valley. The spores will always be lodged on the nerve endings in my nose.

Tónio got paper towels and a bucket and mop, and while he began sponging the rug my father said, "Shall I give the patient my good night blessing? It's early yet, but he should rest."

"My father wants to know if you'd like his good night blessing," I said to Mateus, whose eyes were shut. "Would you like that? Did your parents give you one when you were small?"

His head shook and I couldn't tell if he meant yes or no. I went through the exercise of transplanting one phone and propping the other at Mateus's ear. Tónio was running a faucet, rinsing the mop. Mateus curled on his side so he could listen without the exertion of holding the phone. A glycerin finish was brimming back onto his dull skin. *In the name of the Father . . .*

I couldn't focus for a second. The room smelled like a person disemboweled, poured inside out, and I was sure I'd faint. I revived at . . . *Ghost. May God bless you and make you a biiiiig saint . . .*

Had it been thirty years since I'd last heard that warbling play with *muito grande* until—*I* after *I* after *I*—it stretched accordion-wide? *Good night, sleep well, young man.*

Mateus tried to speak but he was too undone. I told my father something to the effect that he was beyond words. Before I hung up the phone I said, "Thank you, Dad. Good night. Good night."

Mateus passed out while I was helping Toninho reswab the floors, filling the place with the pungent smell of a hospital. Already the remainder of our fried fish was looking like tarnishing bronze; the pineapple was exuding its insides. We hadn't eaten much, but we were no longer hungry. I blew out the candles and Tónio and I worked without speaking in the kitchen, washing plates, drying them. Of course Mateus would have the instincts of someone who shows up to offer help once the work is done, and the very second I was putting away the last plate we heard him call out hoarsely, "Cat, the phone, if you please!" He was languishing regally against the cushions. "I must thank your father, now that I have a voice."

"Big of you," said Tónio, bringing him the phone and setting me up with my connection, "since it's his bill in both directions, pá."

Mateus hauled my father out of his own nap; he was groggy.

"Senhor!" Mateus croaked. "You sound sleepy! Allow me to sing the Ducky Song to put you to rest."

"Heavens, won't that be soothing," said my father. "On one condition. You will tell me why you cannot speak to your parents."

"Ai, well," said Mateus, shifting around. "They have their religion, they push it down my throat, I choke on it, that's the story."

"Have you read Tolstoy? I've just reread *Anna Karenina*."

"Who? No," said Mateus.

"I am at the part, near the end, where the fathers are speaking of the difficulty of creating children, saying that the struggle to train them is so endless that no one can think of bringing them up by his strength alone, and that is where religion comes in."

"Fathers drive their children away."

"Yes," said my father. "They send them off, it's true. They are frightened at how they want them near."

"If I go home," said Mateus, "I suppose my reward will be great in heaven, for putting up with their need to think they're good to me?"

"How should I know if there's a heaven?" said my father. "The reward will be on earth for you. That is the certainty. This is a chance for you to change your history. Sometimes grown-ups do what they should, not what they want."

"I don't see how this is any of your—"

"Let me put it to you another way."

I pressed the receiver closer to my ear.

"If you do not give the gift of yourself to your parents, if you miss this chance to be an adult, you will perish in my rooms as a homeless soul. I can't return to my country in this lifetime, so it will be up to my soul to go back where it belongs. But if you die there a wanderer, you will haunt my place."

Tónio arranged himself to sit behind me on the floor, his legs in a grasshopper-bend around my sides. His arm pinned me to the front of him.

Mateus said, "I'll think about it. Will that be sufficient?"

"Good," said my father. "Torment me now, patient dad that I am, with the Ducky Song."

Mateus didn't hit high C or his magical spot above it. The tune didn't require that, even if his throat could have managed it.

All the little ducks have finished playing
Finished playing . . .
It is the hour for them to go to sleep . . .
Go to sleep . . . Turn out the light. Turn out the light.

But his singing vaulted during the phrase *a-CAB-am de brincar* and ricocheted into me, and the echo made by the impact chimed outward.

Tónio took the phone and said, "Senhor Alberto? I wish we had met. Cat and I, we are good friends. She is stubborn, as you know, but smart, and she will be able to take care of herself. I can promise you that, Senhor Alberto. Our patient here is fine, and thanks to your instructing me I am fine also, very fine."

When I managed a good-bye to my father, he said, in parting, "No more fighting. Buy carnations for the dying young man. I can't fight anyone's need for peace."

I replied faintly that the corner market would be open.

The evening was glistening. Tónio and I set out; disinfectant coursed like liquid moon through the cracks in the sidewalk. I'd have thought that my father's years as a nurse would have put him off carnations—that pungent odor of the water they decay in!

We greeted Esteves, the owner of the Canto Belo, and brought him a dripping armful of carnations from the bucket set in front, under the awning, by the bins of dates and walnuts. From a spool of pearl-gray ribbon he tied a bow around my carnations, and he rasped the blade of a scissors on the ribbon to curl it.

"Ah!" said Esteves. He had a gold molar and an immaculate apron and a pocked complexion, like the top of an overboiled custard, that spoke of a deathly shy adolescence. On display were girls' jewelry boxes, with the ballerinas intact but the musical gears extracted to exhibit the ground spices.

Esteves's shop wafted a perfume of cloves, mace, and allspice as I took Toninho's arm and stepped with my bouquet into the street, where we stood together, arrested.

Women were leaning over windowsills, looking altogether like open flaps in an Advent calendar.

A billboard was advertising the Lalique exhibit at the Gulbenkian Museum. The pictures of milk-colored cameos throbbed like pure light.

A hobbled man with a lion's head cane undertook the extreme exertion required to lift his homburg and wish us a good evening. Out of his smoke-damaged throat issued, "I see that a flower is carrying flowers. You are a bride."

My father's plea for peace unlatched the lockbox in me where his old stories lay. In 1974 Lisboans listened for a song on the radio as a signal to go into the streets when the dictatorship was teetering. A woman who had not sold her flowers that day began sticking carnations into the gun barrels of soldiers. Everyone followed suit, helping to speed to an end, with the force of flowers, a reign of oppression.

My father wasn't having me bring Mateus carnations because they were hospital flowers; they were signaling my father's surrender. Mateus could stay as long as he liked. He'd get to decide. It was a last pleasure for my father to converse on the level of deep history, native son to lateral native son, and a last pleasure for me, perhaps, that he trusted me to interpret his language. A beat or two late, but I'd gotten it. My father had not been present for the Carnation Revolution; he'd only watched the newsreels on the Luso channel at home—one of the rare occasions when he'd allowed himself to succumb to television.

If he protested when I showed up, I'd quote back to him his line about parents being too frightened to say they wanted their children near. That was how I would read the carnation story back to him: peace had arrived when people declared, All of us will face what we must face, even if we perish together.

As Toninho fit my key into the building's front door, I glanced between the parted drapes of the porteira and saw her in a torso-sheathing apron decorated with daisies. Rock-bodied, shelf-breasted, in her cat's-eye glasses, she was feeding a baby in a high chair. A woman slightly under my age was sitting pretzel-limbed on a stool: leg spiraling around her other leg, arms that would complete a perfect straitjacketed pose if she weren't puffing a cigarette. The unwed daughter. The two women caught me spying. I'd once come across Deolinda pawing through my trash to bolster her contempt for prodigal Americans, but her daughter pitched a friendly wink at us through the glass.

When I set the carnations in a vase on Mateus's nightstand, he plucked out one and handed it back. He could comprehend how my father was talking to him. I said, "I'll leave in the morning. You'll need your rest."

"Tell your father they are my favorite plant," he said. "Good night, green-eyed lady. I'm going to die with your kindness on me."

I reserved, at a staggering cost, a seat on a morning plane. Tónio promised to stay with Mateus until there'd be no putting off the hospital. And he'd finish the sale of the apartment without me. I called my father to say I'd be racing home.

"That would be a good idea," he said. "I'd like that, Catarina."

"It's almost Christmas, Dad. I'm going to take care of you whether you like it or not." The cord of the phone swayed and quavered. Sometimes creation itself speaks out of a deep silence, to say: *This is the true story.* Tell us how your love will deliver us all to a heaven you have made. For everyone, including God the Father Himself, needs a father, a mother, a sister and brother, and that is why He invented you.

Toninho snored that night next to me while I stayed flat on my back. The hours dissolved without my knowing it. I woke in the dark, when it's hard to guess the time. Tónio stirred gently as well. He sat up and scrubbed at his face with his hands as I went to the window and lifted the blinds. I suspected it was five in the morning, an hour I worship; the sky pounds the black pearl of the night until it is in pieces and for a brief time, right then, the white of day is the grout holding it together, a perfect tiled mosaic to greet us, the hour that's the artwork most like making love, opposites fixed all the way up to heaven.

But then the beauty of it dissolves.

Tónio joined me in regarding the sky. I clutched his hand as we stared straight ahead. "Honey pie, that nun you wrote about," he said. "I'm afraid she's you. I'm afraid you're turning into one of those pretty women who's sad, and you'll fold yourself up and up and I won't be able to find you anymore." He asked me if I was aware of the quote by Claude Lévi-Strauss, *I am the place in which something has occurred.*

I said I was glad to learn it.

"Well, OK, Cat," he said, kissing my left palm. He got doubly gleeful whenever he landed on a bookish fact I didn't know. "I think I am the place in which *someone* has occurred. That is you."

I stretched my arms toward his neck to hold him and said he was my country, too.

I also noticed the mute alarm clock.

Time to leave.

When my flight was called Tónio reached into his breast pocket to give me a comb as a gift. It had hammered gold oak leaves finely tooled with veins, arranged on the tortoiseshell spine so that, if I were standing outside, or at a window, the sunlight would snag on the edges of the leaves and drip its blood, and the back of my head would throw out spokes of autumn red. I dashed myself onto the shoal of his neck as he started to wail. He understood it was likely to be an indefinite while before I returned in the flesh, that I was the type made comatose by events. He'd grasped long before me that grief begins as a crawling and wailing thing, and then it grows older. The second and endless half of grief is quiet, because the best part of you gets spirited away and, rage extracted, undone—why most people begin to figure from the calm of you that you're just about happy.

One month to the day before Mateus followed suit, my father died. Tónio reported that the date of my father's death coincided with Mateus asking to be taken to his parents. He stayed in his boyhood room and endured his mother's scoldings and his father's silence. He never made it to a hospital; he died at home, and Tónio was with him. I wish my father had known this before he passed away. Toninho thereafter concluded the apartment's sale to the widow of the Communist leader for her granddaughter. My niece and two nephews each have a modest sum that college will eat up.

But the granddaughter suffered a compound fracture of the leg soon after moving in and took it as an omen that she should be healed by moving to the sea. She negotiated with her grandmother to sell the place for a profit to her divorced cousin, who happened to be the head chef at a three-star restaurant not far from the Castelo de São Jorge. Tónio was irked at a summons to show the apartment, but soon thereafter he moved in with the chef, Bartolomeu, who had custody of his ten-year-old son.

The house is crowded, querida, but I am glad. The porteira had quit radiating disapproval, since Bartolomeu brought her cash but also trays of food, including a menagerie of creampuff animals under a spun-sugar cage.

Cat . . . our home is really yours . . . Come when you can! But also I carry you around wherever I go, you are so very light.—Your Senhor T.

I managed a final outing with my father, to the Japanese Tea Garden. It was one of those strange last days when he seemed on the mend. We ordered jasmine tea and fortune cookies and rested with the scent of the old redwood bridge still strong near the bamboo. He'd taught me how to paint bamboo on paper, with black ink, in segments made with single, firm gestures aiming to convey a lifetime of knowledge. *Don't worry your lines. Just draw them, dear.*

My fortune read, "You will meet a tall, dark stranger."

"I can't deal with this," I said. "This couldn't be for me." I handed him the slip of paper.

"Oh, yes." His grin was a marvel that drew in his whole face. "The busy gentleman with the scythe."

I grabbed the fortune from my dad's hand and put it in my teacup and dowsed it with the last of the lavender-tinged water.

Without moving his head, his vision went from the oleander and dragon statues and carried itself past where we were, into the far manzanita and vents in the desert, the screech of the steam spraying from the center of the earth.

"Dad?" It was the first time in all our lives that I was bringing up the subject with him. "They were probably trying to frighten you by yelling in the back room. For writing about better medicine. That's what Mama said. But they didn't frighten you, not so much, did they?"

He finished his jasmine tea and studied the dregs of the leaves. "No, I'm afraid that's not the case," he said. "Look, promise me you won't let anyone hurt you. Because I love you like mad."

"Don't worry about me. I love you, too."

"There's no mistaking that scream. It's too raw. It can't be faked. That high note. If you try intellectually to scream like that, you can't. It's like the difference between what's real and genuine, and what you pretend might be real."

The pot of tea was finished, but I made the gesture of pouring.

"There's a sound all creatures make when they've been inflicted with a mortal wound. It goes into your head like an arrow and stays."

His stare left the far plains and came back, to be with me for a little while more.

I paid for my father to be transported to a private room at Children's Hospital. At first I thought it was my gift to him, but then I saw it was his gift to me, for him to be a child as I held the covered plastic glass of water with its straw for him to drink. I sat by his bedside, folding cranes. Stringing a thousand of them for a wedding is meant to call upon joy. It gave me something to do so I could bear the agony of his drugged breathing, his gazing at me until we both had to look away.

"Allow me, Catarina," he said, and I handed him a square of golden paper and his hands stopped shaking as he shaped the beak of a crane with a perfectly mitered point. I'd been folding in a hurry, but he moved slowly so the edges were exactly met. He was beaming as he handed his work of art over to me.

He had stayed here overnight many times in his career. When an orphan named Eddie Martinez was dying, my father was with him in the final week, sleepless on a cot next to him, alert to the little boy's cries; on other occasions he'd nap in the hallway and spring up when pain made the children bellow from a distant room.

But he would not cry out himself. He would not alarm the dozing of the night nurse.

"Papa," I said, smoothing his spare white hair out of his eyes. He looked straight into mine. *"Deus o abençoe e o faça um santo muiiiiito grande. Boa noite, durma bem,"* I said.

God bless you and make you a biiiiig saint. Good night, sleep well.

That was when I felt his spirit detaching from the loosening paste of his skin, to burrow inside and wrap his soul to carry him away. I knew he'd wait until I was gone to attend to the business of dying. David had come and gone, quickly, but that was how my father preferred it. He'd said earlier he would always be with me, it wouldn't matter where he was traveling now.

As I leaned down to kiss my father's forehead, he kissed my chin. That was how the night blessing played itself out. You asked for a kiss to take with you, especially since you or he might not wake; who knew what fate would bring? And then I said what the parent might utter in a still further closing to the child, the equivalent of how we wish someone sweet dreams, the thing he'd left off saying to me when I was fourteen: *Sonhos cor-de-rosa.*

Pink dreams. Go to the land where you dream in color.

I'd found him a set of pajamas covered with whales and dolphins, something sporty for a large teenager. I stood framed in the doorway to give him a last picture, and he turned his head to watch me leave. It is never too late to save someone, to grant him peace. It is never too late to save yourself by saving someone. I smiled and so did he, and then all that was left for me was to leave him and imagine his journey; it was beginning. The marine animals around his remains were floating at the ready to coast him that night across the sea, to wash up on the shore of his long-lost earthly home, and from there to lift as fallen rain does in an exaltation of quiet back to the wide blue sky.

In the Prairie Schooner Book Prize in Fiction series

Last Call
By K. L. Cook

Carrying the Torch
By Brock Clarke

Nocturnal America ·
By John Keeble

The Alice Stories
By Jesse Lee Kercheval

*Our Lady of the Artichokes and
Other Portuguese-American Stories*
By Katherine Vaz

UNIVERSITY OF NEBRASKA PRESS

Also of interest in the Prairie Schooner Book Prize in Fiction series:

Carrying the Torch
Stories
By Brock Clarke

The stories in this collection occupy a world at once as familiar as a suburban backyard or a southern college's hallowed football field and as strange as a man who buys Savannah, Georgia, and tries to turn it into the perfect Southern city as part of his attempt to win back his estranged wife.

ISBN: 978-0-8032-1551-1 (cloth)

Nocturnal America
By John Keeble

This collection of loosely connected tales returns readers to the American Northwest so finely observed and powerfully evoked in John Keeble's previous, celebrated works. *Nocturnal America* occupies a terrain at once familiar and strange, where homecoming and dislocation can coincide, and families can break apart or hone themselves on the hard edges of daily life.

ISBN: 978-0-8032-2777-4 (cloth)

The Alice Stories
By Jesse Lee Kercheval

Wisconsin is not where Alice, a girl raised in Florida, meant to end up. But when she falls in love with Anders Dahl, a descendant of Norwegian farmers born for generations in the same stone farmhouse, she realizes that to love Anders is to settle into a life in Wisconsin in the small house they buy before their daughter, Maude, is born. Together, Alice and Anders move forward into a life of family, friends, and the occasional troubled student until they face their biggest challenge.

ISBN: 978-0-8032-1135-3 (cloth)

Order online at www.nebraskapress.unl.edu or call 1-800-755-1105. When ordering mention the code BOFOX to receive a 20% discount.